TRISKAIDEKAN

13 STORIES FOR 2013

Proudly Presented By

WWW.COLUMBUSCOOP.ORG

Edited By
Brenda Layman & Brad Pauquette

Pauquette ltd
dba Columbus Creative Cooperative
P.O. Box 91028
Columbus, OH 43209
www.ColumbusCoop.org

DEVELOPMENTAL EDITOR
Brad Pauquette

COPY EDITOR
Brenda Layman

PRODUCTION EDITOR
Brad Pauquette

Cover design by Brad Pauquette
Cover photograph by Melissa Pauquette

Print ISBN 978-0-9835205-8-0
Ebook ISBN 978-0-9835205-9-7

Printed in the United States of America
1 3 5 7 9 10 8 6 4 2

To the new year, 2013. May it bring a change of luck.

CONTENTS

I think we consider too much the good luck of the early bird and not enough the bad luck of the early worm.

-Franklin D. Roosevelt

INTRODUCTION

If you're reading this book, then I've got good news and I've got bad news.

The good news is that, apparently, the world did not end on December 21, 2012 with the completion of the thirteenth Mayan baktun.

The bad news is that if you're triskaidekaphobic, you're about to get a whirlwind of therapeutic treatment that may exceed your comfort level.

In preparation for the year 2013, we put out a call to short story writers in Ohio and across the globe to give us their best work that referenced the number 13. We received a variety of stories, and they truly took the number thirteen in every conceivable direction, from references to time, place and number, to the philosophical value of the number itself.

We selected thirteen stories, and, as usual, we found enough exceptional stories written by Ohio authors, that we used work from the great buckeye state exclusively.

When you read this book and share it with your friends, family and neighbors, you're supporting individual artists in the Central Ohio community, and you're helping them, in a very real way, to take steps towards their dream.

You'll find your fair share of tales of misfortunate anti-heroes and unlucky catalysts, but you'll also find uplifting adventure, romance, historical fiction, drama, creative non-fiction and more in the pages of this work.

Thank you for reading our book. Thank you for supporting the Central Ohio community of artists.

We hope you enjoy this book of thirteen stories about the number 13, and we hope it accentuates what could be a very long year.

To those triskaidekaphobes, buckle your seatbelts, it's about to get real.

-Brad Pauquette
Director, Columbus Creative Cooperative

Triskaideka is a prefix referring to "thirteen," as in triskaidekalets (thirteen babies), triskaidekacycle (a vehicle with thirteen wheels), and triskaidekaphobia (the fear of the number 13).

For more information about Columbus Creative Cooperative and to learn more about our other anthologies of local literature, please visit us at
www.ColumbusCoop.org

PATTERNS
BY KELSEY LYNNE

I shared my house with a woman. I could not say that we were together, not since the storm started, but she was in my house and neither of us were willing to admit that this thing between us was broken. These were the last days of the earth and it seemed like a wasted gesture to have that conversation. Our tomorrows were numbered. What was one more day of a facade, of tip-toeing around the dark rooms of the house, avoiding each other's eyes and shying away each time our hands went for the same piece of glassware or went to close the curtains at the window?

There were bottles everywhere, lining the walls, stacked in orderly piles in the basement on the concrete slab. Thin plastic milk jugs, glass mason jars, beer bottles re-sealed with duct tape—anything that could hold liquid had been filled with what little water was left in the world and put away. Other houses were doing the same, she said, and we had to be prepared for when the city water shut down entirely and we were on our own. She built a solar still in the backyard, but it would not work, so she scavenged. The grocery stores had already been emptied. She still went to them, sometimes, in the middle of the night and stepped through the shattered windows to walk the dark aisles and stare at the empty shelves, as if she thought she would find one last gallon of water that everyone else had missed.

I used to tell her she was wasting her time, that it was dangerous to

3

go outside in the storm, with civilization crumbling bit by bit around us. I didn't bother anymore. This was a slow death, we were not dying in a final apocalyptic blaze of pain and terror, but rather we were wasting away in pieces. Civilization was not going to burn. It was going to give up in weariness, turn over in its bed and go to sleep. The woman in my house was plodding to the end of it all like the rest of us, but she would not speak of it, just as we would not speak of each other.

We spoke of other things. We discussed rations and what little news managed to punctuate the static in the air. Rumors talked of salvation on the west coast or on the east coast or overseas—little sanctuaries hollowed out in defiance of the storm. There was no way to know if this was true and if we had heard the rumors, so had everyone else. She still asked, sometimes, if we should go and try to make it to one of these places where they said we could survive. I sensed it was more for the sake of conversation—anything but what was no longer between us— and did not answer her one way or another. We had made that decision already. Instead, I told her of the patterns I saw in things when I went outside. The way the dust swirled across the sidewalk and how it was sometimes brushed aside, like the wind was a hand clearing out a space to see the asphalt and dead grass that lay underneath. I saw circles in those moments, dozens of small circles eddying about like living things before the wind blew the sand back over it and covered the patterns up. I saw in her eyes that she was afraid of the way I spoke. In the past, I would have been silent for her sake and kept these patterns and numbers to myself. That was broken now and I no longer cared what she thought of me.

I think that perhaps she saw them too, when I pointed them out. I caught her eyes lingering on the shattered glass in the street, studying how the shards all fell in a circle with the center bare asphalt. How the birds flew in flocks of nine and how the collapsed bridge over the river retained only three of the support pillars, broken fingers in the bracken water. They were everywhere. I broke into the library, at night, not because I feared reprisal—the police force had crumbled by then—but because the sun was too oppressive during the day. It felt like the sun was drawing nearer and even though the scientists had sworn this was not what was happening to our planet, I couldn't help but think they were wrong. It wasn't like anything else made sense anymore. There, alone among the rows of bookcases like silent sentinels, I searched for books on mathematics, on religion. On anything that could explain these patterns and symbols I saw. I brought stacks home that night and the woman in my house watched from the living room, her legs drawn up and her knees tight to her chest, dressed only in a t-shirt and her panties. I wondered if I had woken her coming in and out of the front door and why she did not move, even though each trip to the library took almost half an hour to walk there and back.

My arms were burning by the time I was satisfied and the books littered the entryway in sloppy piles. She stared at them for a long time, like a feral animal backed into a corner, and I tried to explain. I was helpless before her alien eyes and my words fell useless. I was like one of those scientists on the radio, my voice chattering meaningless explanations until static overwhelmed it and the only sound was the whispering of sand against the windows. I gave up and took three of the books to my room with me. Much later, when the sun was high and we had drawn the blackout curtains over the window to keep the sun from baking the interior of the house, I emerged and found that she had toppled my stacks of books, thrown them until they were scattered like leaves across the entryway and living room both. They lay there with broken spines and I walked through the battlefield, examining the fallen, and when I passed into the living room I saw the dents in the wall where the books had struck the plaster and then fallen to the floor. They lay in a trail, like a row of ants, curling into itself. Curious, I climbed onto the back of the sofa and stood there, perched precariously on the furniture, and saw that from above, the trails formed a symbol, a spiral. They'd been thrown and fallen into a spiral.

From the doorway, I could see the woman standing by the sink. Water had stopped working but she stood there anyway, her hands on the porcelain. I could hear in my mind the clink of dishes as we filled the sink, together, after a meal. Now there was silence. I climbed down and walked to her, standing just a foot away, a hand half-raised as to touch her shoulder.

"Listen," she whispered, "I still hear the wind."

It was a wounded beast, its roar merely the death moan as it bled sand across the entire world. It would bury us, turn the rivers and oceans into mud, a never-ending sandstorm that would wipe all life off the face of the planet while the hostile sun drew ever nearer, threatening to swallow us whole. There were no explanations for this. It simply was. And there was a spiral in our living room, made out of human knowledge, and the wind continued unabated.

I dropped my hand and walked away. It was only much later, after I had re-stacked the books in the entryway, that I realized there had been no sand in the wind that rattled the panes of our windows. For that handful of moments when the woman stood by the window, I had not heard the constant scratch of sand against the walls of our house.

I continued my search. I wrote notes. I learned what the Fibonacci sequence was, I filled two sheets of notebook paper with the digits of pi. I took glasses in the kitchen out of the cupboard and set them on the table in series of prime numbers. When the woman found them later, she moved them to rest on windowsills in straight lines with no seeming reason behind the number of glasses she set on each window. She wandered aimlessly from room to room that day, then around evening, she returned to the windows and I saw that she had changed the numbers so that each one had only nine glasses. Tiny shot glasses in the kitchen, wine glasses in the living room, plastic cups in the bathroom. I stood behind her as she set up the ones in the bedroom, watching.

"Like the birds," I finally said. She started and turned, her elbow catching on the blackout curtains and drawing them forward for a moment. One of the glasses tumbled as the cloth caught it and she stared at it on the carpet so that she did not have to look at me.

"It looks nice when they're ordered," she said, "and if you're going to insist on—on fucking up the house, then it might as well look nice."

She pushed past me into the hallway and I heard her footsteps heavy on the stairs.

"Like the birds," I repeated. The storms had grounded the planes but they had not killed the birds and like everything else, no one could explain why.

She saw. I know she did.

The storm had driven humanity indoors and underground. People were dying now and there was violence in the streets. It had not spread to where we lived, not yet, but everyone knew it was coming. I saw it in how the neighbors watched the windows and how fewer people went out at night. We had all wandered the streets aimlessly before, watching the sky, hoping to see a star bloom behind all the sand. Humanity gathered in churches and temples and sent desperate prayers up to a sky that had turned against us; we met in deserted parking lots and exchanged what bits of news we could find. Now, that was all gone, and we stayed in our houses and the churches remained empty save for the few that had truly given up and were simply waiting to die.

We had no guns and the woman in my house worried about this. She vanished one night without a word and I waited up for her, uncertain as to why I was making the gesture. The glasses in the window caught the light from the single candle I had lit against the darkness. When she returned she slunk in through the backdoor like a teenager trying not to get caught by her parents. I saw that she carried a shotgun in her hands and a backpack across one shoulder. She was trembling like a leaf and it took three tries before she managed to slide the chain into place on the door. There was a strange smell on the air that I couldn't place at all, something that I was not familiar with. The scent seemed faintly metallic, buried underneath the stink of gun oil.

"Where did you get that?" I asked softly and she almost dropped the gun with a scream. Then she put her back against the door and sucked in breath, drawing the features of her face back to a semblance of calm.

"I found it," she said and her voice was trembling.

She seemed on the verge of saying something more. I heard the words in my head. We needed a weapon. We had to protect ourselves, there would be violence soon enough in our city and our house was not defensible on its own. People would turn against each other, we were descending into savagery, and the only thing that mattered now was the two of us. These were her justifications.

I stood and blew out the candle so she would not have to say these words. I left her there to stow the gun somewhere safe and close at hand. In the morning, I did not ask her about the grime beneath her fingernails and whether it was grease or blood or both. Her justifications were enough for me. I had only my numbers and symbols and here she had brought food and water and now a weapon. What had my hands done?

Later, I went to the doors leading out of the house and drew spirals until the doors were covered with black marker. Each one conformed to the Fibonacci sequence. She watched me as I did this.

"They look like flowers," she said, "Or seashells."

"The pattern is found everywhere in nature. It forms the honeybees' family tree, even."

"It's disturbing."

It was the first conversation in a long time. I could not say for how long, as time had lost its meaning, and we had no mechanical clocks to tell us what hour of the day it was.

Later—some days later—we heard gunshots. She stood by the window, carefully against the wall, peering through a tiny crack in the curtains for a long time, shotgun in hand. The gunshots continued throughout the day intermittently, but they never came near our house. I saw her tracing the patterns in the door with her finger when it was all done and it had been quiet for some time, and then she broke down weeping. I risked touching her, my fingers on the back of her head, and was surprised by the feel of her hair. Slick, unpleasant. It was not as I remembered and I backed away and let her cry alone.

The storm intensified. On some days it would cut through skin, the sand leaving furrows on exposed flesh, like the wind had been given claws. It broke a window in our house, shattering the glass in one burst, and we both raced to the source of the crash. She carried the shotgun and there was a cartridge in the chamber. The glass lay blown in across the kitchen floor and the shot glasses she had lined up were untouched on the sill. For a moment we just stood there, staring at it, hearts pounding. I counted my pulse as it roared in my ears. Five. Seven. Nine. Then she shivered into life.

"It doesn't work," she said, walking past me and putting the shotgun on the counter, "it didn't work."

She swept the shot glasses off the sill with the back of her hand. They shattered on the floor, one by one, like gunshots made of glass. I flinched back, as we were strangers to each other again.

"It didn't work!" she cried and the anger in her voice felt like it was directed at me, as if I was to blame. I was the reason the storm raged, I was the reason she had gone in the night to steal a gun, and I was the reason there was glass all over the floor and sand blowing in through the broken panes.

I fled. I had nowhere to go, but I fled. Out the back door covered in spirals into the small fenced yard, ankle-deep in shifting sand. The grass was all dead, bleached brown, and I wondered what the world would look like when this was all done. Everything hues of tan and khaki with the whites of our bones interred into the endless desert. I sank to my knees, feeling the sand trace the contours of my face. It cut lines into my hands and I saw blood well up in the grooves. I swept my hand out, tracing a line in the sand, until I was surrounded by a circle. The wind did not wipe it away. I knelt there for a long time, considering this, and then I rose and stepped over the boundaries of the circle. It remained. I walked to the fence and found where we had stacked tinder, long ago when winter was a reality. From this, I took sticks, and I walked the perimeter of our house and once I had paced out a circle, I did the math in my head, and retraced my steps. At certain intervals I paused and dug a stick into the ground. When I was finished, there were seven in all, making a perfect circle around the house. Then I went inside.

We remained strangers. I thought that perhaps she despised me and so I avoided her gaze, wondering how long it would be before we turned on each other. Our water was running low and each night, once the sun no longer bore down upon us like a furnace, she crept outside to check the solar still. Futile hope. Even I had given up on my patterns, idly tracing circles in the sand that had blown into the entryway without any real expectation of change. Nothing made sense, not even my numbers and patterns now.

Then, one evening, she returned with water. Her face was drawn and she did not cry—we did not have enough water to spare for such a gesture—but I saw a faint glimmer in her eyes. It wasn't quite hope. It wasn't quite feral madness. It was something else, a curiosity perhaps, and I looked at the jar she held in her hands. There was three inches of water in it. Neither of us spoke. She added it to our dwindling supply and I went out back and gathered sticks. Then, I walked down the empty street, the asphalt long buried under the sand, and drove seven sticks in a circle around each of our neighbor's houses. I no longer knew who remained and who lived, but I walked the entire block, and when I was done I went back inside. I wondered if anyone watched me from their curtained windows and if they understood or even cared.

The next night, I went out with a marker and drew spirals on the outside of each door along our block. One of the neighbors came out and watched me from his porch, but he made no move to approach. I did not recognize him. The woman I lived with would know; she knew everyone it seemed. Before the sand. Before the storm.

"It's not going to be enough," the woman said one day, "The solar still traps enough to keep us alive, but we're going to run out of food."

"We have seeds. I'll put up a shade and we can plant."

"There's not enough water in the soil and your sticks won't change that."

"Then I'll—"

"It's not going to work!"

We had spoken in hushed tones or not at all for so long that her exclamation startled me. I saw a woman worn thin in that moment, as thin as the world had become and as thin as my own spirit was. Scraped clean by the endless sand. It would have been easier if we'd just lain on the ground and let the sand swallow our bones; this constant fighting with the elements was destroying us in pieces. I envied the dead.

"I've done everything," I whispered, "Holy numbers and patterns repeated throughout nature…what else is there?"

She sucked in a sharp breath. I saw her body focus, intent on something her mind was chasing through the internal paths of her mind. Then she moved, toward the door, and I moved to stop her as it was still day, but she moved too quickly and the door banged open before her. I stood in the doorway, watching, afraid to follow. She braced herself against the wind, shoulders hunched and back bent, and I watched as she approached the dwindling pile of kindling and took a number of branches from it. Then she struggled to the ring of seven sticks. I dared to follow, feeling the wind claw at my face and hiss in my ears. The sun was like passing my hand over a lighter, an inch closer and I would be burned up.

She stabbed the first stick in the ground with such violence that I thought it would break in her hand. It stood there at a lopsided angle, breaking the symmetry of my circle, and then she moved to the side and placed another. And another. I counted as she did—nine, ten. Thirteen. Then she was done and she came inside, her eyes daring me to say something. Anything at all. To refute her or proclaim it all hopeless.

I saw then, where her mind had gone. Everything about this was unnatural; it defied religion and science both, so now she turned to unnatural means. A contrary number, a pattern that was broken, to refute a broken world.

That night, we slept in relative quiet. The wind only caressed our windows.

That morning, the solar still was full, and there were sprouts of green in our backyard. We planted the seeds, side by side, in small rows and when our hands brushed neither of us recoiled at the touch.

· 13 ·

Kelsey Lynne is an automated testing developer. She enjoys writing in her free time, typically between the hours of twelve and one AM. When she is not coding or depriving herself of sleep to write, she enjoys painting and playing the harp. Her education consists of a bachelor's in computer science and two years of a creative writing minor, before she changed her minor to business so she could take exciting classes—like Finance 101. Kelsey lives with her three cats and one dog.

THIRTEEN VISITS
TO THE SAME STATE

BY DREW FARNSWORTH

D eacon tapped at his glass of Diet Coke. Second dates weren't his forte. Fifth or sixth maybe—though he would probably hit his stride around ten or twelve.

Fei, on the other hand, usually got to know the person on the other side of the table instantly. Deacon was still an enigma though. Maybe that was how he got to the second date.

"Deacon," Fei began as she echoed his tapping against her own glass to taunt him. "You have deep eyes. Has anyone ever told you that?"

The tapping stopped for both of them. Deacon looked away and blushed. He brushed a hand through his hair. "Something like that, I guess."

They smiled politely and took small bites from their respective burgers. The little bistro wasn't crowded, but for a Wednesday night it wasn't quite dead. The perfect setting, probably, for a second date. A quiet, dim place with enough noise to convince you that no one listened in.

"I'm not good with my eyes," Deacon said. After a dumbstruck look from Fei he fumbled, "I mean I'm not a visual person." Then he gulped down some more Diet Coke. After building up some courage he said, "I think thoughts are more beautiful than images anyway."

"Oh," Fei sighed. "Maybe your eyes are meant to be seen more

13

than they're meant to see." She snuck a furtive napkin wipe at a bit of ketchup on the corner of her mouth. "So what's the most beautiful thought you've ever had?"

Deacon stopped cold, even though he knew his answer outright. He tried to look casual. This was one of those questions one asks to try to evoke depth even though one isn't actually prepared to dive in that deeply. He sometimes made the mistake of taking questions like this at face value. He thought better of it and shrugged. "I forget."

"Oh," Fei sighed again. The smooth skin of her cheeks puckered against the corners of her eyes. "You can't say it's the most beautiful thought you've ever had and then say you forget it. That doesn't make any sense."

Deacon fidgeted. "I see your point," he groaned. He looked into the distance and mused. "I've had this feeling a lot. Always in the same situation. I'll do my best to explain." He wiped his mouth with little pats at the corners then brushed a hand against his five o'clock shadow. At his age it took two days to mature. "So you've read about propofol, right? I think we had a question about it on the Pharmacology test last semester. It's a twilight agent. You experience the surgery but you can only remember bits and pieces.

"It puts you in this dream state where you're experiencing the world but not the way you normally would." He thought for a moment. "So I had this procedure. They put in the IV," he continued, "and I'm sitting there talking, feeling the whole time like I'm in the moment, in control, completely aware. I'm answering questions, I'm making jokes, I'm the life of the O.R...."

Fei laughed tenderly. Deacon smiled too, more at ease than he'd expected. "So they start the procedure and I start thinking about something beautiful, something that I'd known my entire life but couldn't remember. There was pain but it was this sublime pain, this beautiful recognition of my body and my mind and the way they intermixed with the Universe. And there was this one thought. I told myself that I had to remember it. But then after the surgery it was gone." Against his better judgment, his mouth kept moving. "The procedure was a colonoscopy," he said, regretting it long before the words left his mouth. "But it also kind of happened when I had my wisdom teeth out and one time when someone fed me a pot brownie by accident."

They each drank a sip from their drink. Deacon blushed brightly. Fei looked quizzical. "I'm not sure what that story says about you. Does it mean that you live for things you can't have?"

Deacon began to speak but thought better. He dithered through his confusion, adrift in her smile. "No, Fei, I do." He leaned in closer. His lips moved but he couldn't hear what they said. "I'll tell you, Fei, all I'm thinking about right now is how I could bring that smile back."

Fei leaned over her French fries and gave Deacon a little kiss on the cheek.

The 3rd Date

For their third date, Fei and Deacon went to the zoo. It was a quiet day just after finals and before they were scheduled to take the MCATs.

They passed the Panda Paddock. Fei mused softly. "We're in an appropriate section of the zoo, I think."

Deacon looked around for a sign. "What do you mean?"

"Well," Fei answered. "The odds of our going to the same med school are pretty low. Then after that, the odds we get the same internship, the same residency, the same anything, they're low too."

"So, like the pandas we're unlikely to consummate our..." Deacon didn't want to put a word on their relationship. He didn't want to sound too eager or too dismissive.

They walked slowly into a lifeless tree-lined corner of the zoo. The summer pollen blew palpable dusts against their sun ripened cheeks. Deacon wiped a fleck of yellow off of Fei's chin. "You know, you were the one who told me to be in the moment." He smirked and poked her in the shoulder. "And here I am."

"At the zoo," Fei agreed.

"With the wild animals," Deacon noted, gesturing around him toward the seeming wilderness. Without a thought, Deacon cobbled together enough courage, anxiety and gumption to do what he'd never done before. He grabbed Fei's arm and whisked her off into the trees.

The moment grew inside of him and he cautiously followed it into complete oblivion. He'd never let his mind go so fully as he did then. It all happened as if within an instant though they both knew it had been much longer than that. A moment lost to the moment.

Fei laid her head against Deacon's heart.

They breathed softly together, pinned up against a small oak. The dusky sunlight beamed in through the branches, through the pollen and the sodden air as little gusts blew swirls past the leaves.

The 5th Date

They studied too hard to see each other. After the MCATs passed, they both needed to return to their respective home towns and wait for acceptance letters from med school. Their fifth date happened the night before Fei's journey home to Texas. The night sky twinkled as they sat atop Deacon's twenty-five-year-old beat up diesel Mercedes. It was the night of the best meteor shower of the year. They'd driven miles to find an open field.

And had they ever found the place. The Milky Way shown with iridescent fire across the moonless, cloudless sky. They held hands, Deacon gently stroking Fei's with one finger. They'd brought a box of wine, though they weren't drinkers. It was their intent to drink the entire box between them, fall asleep in the luxurious seats of the Benz and open their hearts to fate. Deacon took the first drink and passed the glass to Fei.

An admitted lightweight, Fei drank the glass slowly but with relish. This was a treat. Somehow, she thought, they'd mastered oblivion. They didn't hem and holler about an inexorable future. This was their only night for the rest of eternity.

She caught sight of the first shooting star. Not just a fleeting stripe of glow, it was a line of fire across the sky. Deacon stared into the starlight sparkling on the fine lines of her silken hair. He breathed in the strawberry willowbark tableau of her scent—the sweet spice of her linen blouse.

Fei said, "Let's play a game." She grinned at him. "Here's what you do. You find one star in the sky and you name it. You name it whatever name you want. Name it Juniper or Ugly or Mildred or Confucius. Just name it." She let go of Deacon's leg and fell onto his chest. "Then I'll name a star. Then we start over. We say your star's name then mine and then you name a new star. Then we just keep going until there aren't any stars left to name."

Deacon rolled his eyes. "How do we know we're talking about the same stars? What if my Mildred is your Juniper?"

"I honestly think," Fei began with a portentous gravity bellowing from her diaphragm, "I think at first my Juniper might not be your Juniper, but after time, after a hundred or two hundred names, if we do it right, my Puddleglum will be your Puddleglum. My Bastian will be your Bastian. And we'll definitely have the same Coco."

They started naming stars. It went slowly at first but the speed ramped up so fast that Deacon had trouble keeping track. It came to a head when his seventh turn came. He went through the litany "Juniper, Ugly, Mildred, Confucius, Colin, Pennywise, Poop, Chihuahua, Butch, Cathy, Hui Xu, Stacy and Jack. Now where to put old Spencer?" He looked around and instantly it jumped at him, the perfect spot. A sublime little nook within a cloud of beauty. It was, perhaps, the most perfect spiral within the most focally magnificent center of absolute dark. He told himself he'd never see the sky so brilliant as it was at that moment.

Then a shooting star crossed his eye's path. He blinked. His spot in the sky got lost to the haze of the million billion other stars arrayed like glitter on a black carpet. He wanted to find Spencer again but the moment had passed.

"I see him," Fei blurted. "I see little Spencer."

Deacon's heart jumped. He couldn't find it again. In all the sky he had no idea where little Spencer was. He panicked. Maybe the wine had gotten to him. He didn't even listen as Fei rattled off the names of their stars. He just roiled in his thoughts, kicking himself for having forgotten Spencer yet kicking himself even more for caring. "Do you see Gabbie?" Fei asked. "She's very cute."

Deacon gave up trying. He forgot about the sky and instead focused on the names, neglecting the rules that Fei had laid out. "So we have Juniper, Ugly, Mildred, Confucius, Colin…" and he spun through the names of all those stars without thinking a moment about where they were in the heavens. Once in a while he'd wonder where Spencer was. Spencer was yet another thing he'd thought was so sublime but couldn't remember why or what made it so.

The 7th Date

Deacon and Fei went to different schools. While Fei stayed on the east coast at a well-regarded medical school, Deacon was left to spend his days at a bottom rung school on the outskirts of San Bernardino. They still spoke on occasion. They traded Facebook messages from time to time. They absently kept abreast of each other's relationship statuses as they clicked on from "single" to "in a relationship" to "it's complicated" back to "single." It all amounted to the most vague, most impersonal communication, all supposition and circumstance. Fei supposed that it made sense that they should remain this way, foreign to one another. Always knowing that they had something special but never remembering exactly what it was.

Their residencies came and went. After tortured nights and painfully long hours of thankless doctoring they both became respected neurosurgeons.

18

Eight years later, at a conference in New York, they bumped into each other in the hotel lobby. Their plans solidified within moments, a quaint night together to catch up over Pad Thai at Deacon's apartment.

Deacon had become a tried and true New Yorker with a swanky apartment on the lower east side. It sprawled out onto a quaint little roof deck with manicured potted plants and oil lamps. The stars soldiered vainly behind the orange glow of the city. The night darkened as the street cackled with drunks. Fei and Deacon listened quietly and said almost nothing.

"What was it you said to me when we first talked?" Fei asked. "I was so distracted by your eyes I barely listened."

Deacon shrugged. "I think I asked you if you'd brought your text-book. I hadn't read the chapter and forgot my book."

"No," Fei said. "It was poetic. Something you said was deep and dark. You're hypnotizing sometimes."

Deacon feigned embarrassment and stood up to go inside. He cleared the plate of cheese and glasses of wine from the deck. Fei followed cheerfully.

"I remember," she said. "I remember what you looked like. It was one of the only times you were wearing something other than scrubs. A blue checked shirt and jeans. Your hair was shorter around your ears. You were chewing gum." She laughed. "I always remember people's clothes. I had on a bright yellow sun dress and I had a daisy in my hair that I picked on my way to class."

Deacon nodded like a bored parent, a dismissive acceptance. "I bet I said something dumb. Something a million people said before me."

"You meant it," Fei argued. "You thought the book was wrong about anesthetics. That just because you don't remember something… or maybe…No, you said that because some things can't be remembered they're that much more important. You can't rationalize them away. That's what you said. That's when I told you about Jimmy's party. Our first date."

"See, I thought coffee was our first date," Deacon countered.

"Coffee?" Fei rolled her eyes. "When did we ever have coffee?" she took a deep gulp from her wine. "Look, we've been on seven dates including this one. Isn't that right?"

Deacon nodded. "Sure," he said, trying and failing to count. "Seven."

As the night got colder they went inside to the couch. Fei climbed on top of Deacon and looked him square in the eye. Deacon found his hands in the small of her back. "What are we doing here, Fei?" he asked.

She smiled and kissed him deeply.

Deacon's memory stirred. The feeling of Spencer the star echoing the feeling of the zoo echoing the feeling of the forest echoing the dollop of ketchup on Fei's finger on their second date. A rill flowing through him, building momentum. They connected, those moments. It went back even further and further. Within Fei's lips he felt a connection to something deep and spiritual.

She pulled away and slumped back in a daze. He wanted to explain the feeling but it was already gone. They stared at each other, both of them frightened.

"I think maybe I should get some sleep," Fei pretended to yawn. "I have a big day tomorrow. I'm giving a lecture on temporary stents in the choroidal artery to alleviate thrombosis."

Deacon nodded out of courtesy.

"I know you'll forget all about this," Fei said. "I'll guarantee you that."

Deacon nodded. "I suppose that's how it works." He chuckled to himself as he stood up and got her jacket. "You've got a knack. You're like a drug or a dream. A crossword puzzle I forget about five minutes after I'm done. The blanks just fill themselves in."

Fei opened the door. "With disappearing ink, Deacon."

They kissed in the threshold. Deacon's legs melted beneath him. He said in a dizzy swirl, "We could be good together."

20

Fei grabbed him by the shoulder as if to dance and pulled him in close. They kissed loudly, bumping into walls and crashing down to their knees. If someone saw them they'd have been horrified by the unrepentant abandon. It was ludicrous, uncomfortable ferocity. Like something out of a nature film.

Fei rose first. Deacon remained on the ground like a newborn, unformed. He stood slowly. His face was red with the carpet pattern. She shook her head and turned around. Deacon spoke softly as she walked away. "I'm not normally like this," he said.

"Good," she yelled after him. She straightened her skirt and her eyes darted around to see if anyone was watching.

He went back into his apartment to stare at the ceiling for the five hours until his next day began.

The ninth and tenth dates happened that same week. Either with some colleagues or by themselves, they spent every night together at dinner or for drinks. They avoided eye contact. Fei felt a jolt when she touched Deacon's hand. There was no more kissing between them. Whatever they had that night in Deacon's apartment, they shied away from tempting that feeling again.

The 11th Date

They didn't keep up with each other. For twenty more years they went about their business as neurosurgeons on opposite coasts. Fei moved up the ranks slowly while Deacon flourished in the surgical world. He had hands like steel. Deacon married but divorced. Fei never took a husband.

Fei finally caught her big break. She was offered chief of neurosurgery at Providence General in Rhode Island. Very prestigious. On her first day she went to the cafeteria to feel the lay of the land. She saw Deacon at a table in the corner wearing a smart grey suit and an administrator's badge. Beneath his salt and pepper hair he still had the same cautious smirk. He still carried his shoulders pulled back. She walked

21

over to him and sat down.

"I can't believe you're here, Deacon," she said. "It's kismet."

Deacon smiled deeply. "It's truly a pleasure," he said in a ministerial voice. "Did you just start here?"

"I did," she answered coyly. "You didn't have anything to do with that, did you?"

He shrugged knowingly and took a bite of his cafeteria burger and said through a full palate, "I might have."

Fei looked into those deep eyes. She wondered what she might say. Then she just burst out with it. "I've thought about you."

Deacon shook his head plaintively. "I appreciate that," he said, "but I'm married." He pointed to his ring finger but there was no ring. His finger just looked withered in the place where a ring once had been.

Fei looked at him for a moment. She studied his face. His hands still seemed as rock solid as ever. She told him gently, "Deacon, it's Fei."

"Pardon?" he responded.

"Fei Lao," she said. "From undergrad. From Northwestern hospital."

Deacon studied her face for a full second before a look of understanding crossed his face. "Fei," he cried. "Oh my god, I didn't recognize you!" He swallowed his food and lied, "You look wonderful."

Fei blushed. She put her hand on his. "I'm so happy you're here. You have to tell me all about where you've been and what you've done."

"Well I just got the job here, Fei," he bellowed. "Chief of Neurosurgery at Providence General."

Fei sat back in her chair. "Am I replacing you?" she asked.

"Of course not!" Deacon said, looking at her askance. "I just started six months ago or so. Maybe eight. I'm not good with dates." He smiled and sat back himself. "And only fifteen years out of residency."

Fei's heart dropped. She looked at his badge. He wasn't an administrator. He wasn't even a doctor. He was on the board of directors.

Then she saw on his wrist an admittance band. Not only was he on the board, he was a patient.

Neither spoke for some time.

Then Fei leaned forward and stroked his arm. "We should get together soon," she said. "We have a lot of catching up to do."

Fei learned about Deacon's illness. A benign meningioma located near the hippocampus. It had been there a long time, growing between a hair's width and a millimeter per year. Over thirty years it slowly cut off the blood flow to the hippocampus, disabling bits of his memory at a time. His personality changed. His wife described him as angry, the furthest thing from the Deacon that Fei knew. They took away his medical license but he'd given enough money to keep his place on the board.

Their eleventh date was a quiet dinner in a quiet restaurant. Fei made her introduction to him again and explained that his secretary had made the reservation. He accepted that explanation easily.

He ate a very thick cut of steak while she ate the rice at the corners of her sauce covered plate. "What would you do," she began, "if you had a patient with a benign tumor at the hippocampus that was strangling his anterior choroidal artery? Would you remove it if you had the chance or would you just get rid of the hippocampus to give the tumor room to grow?"

He shrugged and moved into his contemplative medical stance. "Did they perform a Wada test?"

Fei nodded and looked down at her plate. "He'll lose almost all of his memory if we have to remove the left hippocampus."

"But he might get it back if we remove the tumor," Deacon smirked. "You know better than anybody that the brain works in mysterious ways. You never know what you'll lose through surgery. You never know, you might gain."

"The rate of growth for the tumor has increased," Fei continued. "It looks as though it may grow a full three millimeters this year. In that case the artery will be in danger in only a few months."

23

Triskaidekan

Deacon nudged his meal. "So now's the time to operate," he said. "We only get one chance. We either remove the tumor or the hippocampus. It's fifty-fifty that he loses his memory." Deacon looked up at the ceiling and counted to himself. "I've done at least five—maybe seven surgeries in that area. When can we fit him into the schedule?"

Fei took a deep breath. "It's you," she said. "You have the tumor." She nearly cried.

His mouth fell open. He grasped her hand and his lip quivered. They shared breath, the only noise in their minds sounded like the sizzle of bacon and a low, murmuring hum. She squeezed tightly. His muscles loosened. His spirit drifted into the space between their two skins. It lingered there.

Then Deacon smirked, let go of her hand and ate a big piece of gristle. "So get me on the table already," he said. "It's just brain surgery for God's sake." The sound of his chewing chortled across the table. "This is a fantastically delicious steak." He looked around the room and lit up with energy. "It makes sense though," he said. "I have absolutely no clue where I am."

Fei laughed with him. Her pity left her.

The 13th Date

Their twelfth date happened after Deacon formally consented to the surgery. Fei took him out for lunch. She kissed him on the lips when she said goodbye. He pushed her away, still thinking he was married. She'd forgotten to tell him.

She didn't see him again until the day of his surgery. She met him for his prep.

"We'll be administering propofol," she told him plaintively. "I know you know the procedure but I feel like I should explain it anyway."

Deacon smiled in his hospital gown, his shaven head glistening in the fluorescent light. "Sounds good," he said. "You know, they gave me propofol—"

Fei's sad, wet laugh interrupted him. She stroked his hand. "I remember," she said. "You told me years ago."

"Well I'm looking forward to it," he said. "It's an amazing drug, propofol. Instead of making dreams a reality it makes reality a dream."

"It's not a dream," Fei said. She kissed him on the cheek. His warm, stubbled skin caught the grooves of her lips harshly, a tingling reminder of just how real this was.

Deacon brightened like a burning flash. He nodded his head and the drip began.

"What's your sign, Fei?" he asked. They'd begun to administer the local anesthetic but he didn't seem to care. "I'm not good with dates."

"Sagittarius," she answered. "You told me once it was appropriate because part of me is a horse's ass."

Deacon looked into the distance vaguely. "That's a beautiful constellation. It's in such a perfectly brilliant patch of sky. This perfect swirl within the focal point of all astral dark." He laughed hysterically for a moment, his head bobbing back against its restraint. "Spencer," he said. "That's hilarious. That's where Spencer the star lives. Right there in the middle of your sign."

Fei thought he'd fallen into delirium and ignored him.

"It was our fifth date," Deacon continued. "On top of my old rusted Benz." He clicked his tongue. "I wanted so badly to get you into that back seat."

Fei vaguely remembered that night, vaguely remembered playing that star naming game with him. It was so likely a false memory, something he'd fabricated.

"Are you sure you're fit to perform this operation?" he asked. "I mean, you're a competent surgeon, I'm sure…" he bit his tongue. "I don't mean to say…" he clicked his teeth. "But our relationship might cloud your judgment. What does administration tell you? Did George Walker sign off on this?"

"Deacon," Fei began, "George Walker has been dead for three years." She said it matter-of-factly but slowly. Her breath formed a feint omm.

Deacon's eyes darted frantically. "I remember," he said. "It was a Tuesday. June the fourteenth. Molly, that's his wife, she came to the hospital herself, to my office. She told me first. I opened the door to my office and she fell into my arms. She pulled my pocket square out and blew her nose."

Fei looked to the other doctors in the room. This must have been a false memory. Propofol should not counteract loss of memory, she was certain. Perhaps the tumor wasn't the cause of his memory loss. Perhaps it wasn't even physiological. Maybe he'd just repressed his last fifteen years without any alteration to his brain.

One of the half-dozen masked men in the room raised his hand meekly. "It was on a Tuesday," he said. "And I saw her carrying a blue cloth handkerchief."

Deacon laughed again. "That's right. It was cornflower blue. When she gave it back it had a little brown stain from the bloody nose she'd given herself crying. I keep that in my desk drawer to this day. If you hit an artery and I bleed out today…" In cold earnest he stammered, "Not that it would be your fault, Fei. God knows that anterior choroidal artery holds onto those meninges like its life depends on it… my life…" That tongue click popped through the nearly silent operating room. "My point is, Fei, I'd like you to have that…"

Fei laughed back at him. "Don't bequeath me your bloody handkerchief, Deacon. Jesus. Who are you, Othello?"

Deacon didn't even notice as Fei peeled back the layers of skin from his skull. He was just full of laughter. "Oh Shakespeare," he sighed. "That would make you Iago if I'm not mistaken. Or something like that. I was never a very good student. But hell, I took good notes."

Standard procedure in these types of operations involves placing a camera directly in front of the patient's face and projecting his eyes on a giant screen in the corner of the operating room. The theory being that pupil dilation and focal depth are some of the first indicators of brain malfunction. Fei looked straight into his deep, dark eye. "Deacon," she said before she fired up the bone saw. "You'll feel pressure around the…"

"Around the Sutura Squamosa," Deacon interrupted. "I know all about the procedure, Fei. I've done it five times myself."

Fei rolled her eyes. "Around the top of your ear, I was going to say." She poked at the small crevice in his skull. "Do you feel that?"

"You're cutting too close to the sphenoid…"

"Chill out, Deacon," said Fei, finally letting her annoyance show. "I haven't started cutting yet, you backseat driver. In any other situation you can't even commit to a sentence but in this room you're as sure-footed and as stubborn as a mule."

The masked doctor in the background chuckled. He said, "You two sound like an old married couple."

Fei took a breath during the awkward silence that followed. She grabbed the bone saw and carefully made her first cut. She'd done it a hundred times and like each time before she felt the full weight of her patient's life at her fingertips. Deacon stayed silent.

After a bit of procedure, Fei removed the piece of skull to reveal the glistening grey matter beneath with its crystalline lattice of veins and arteries. There sat his temporal lobe and deep inside that his hippocampus. If she damaged this part of the brain during surgery he would almost certainly lose much of his memory. The plan was to poke him with electrodes to assess which areas might be most available for removal if that became necessary.

But first Fei needed to locate the tumor. One entry method was through the nasal cavity but this was ruled out early because of the complexity of the surgery. Instead, Fei entered laterally, right through the side of Deacon's head. This was a common, safe method. Time tested. But the tumor was tucked away right in the middle of Deacon's brain, right at one of the hardest spots to reach. It meant a lot of careful spreading, clamping and prodding to navigate through the small fissures with tiny instruments guided by all kinds of microscopes and scans. She worked slowly, moving almost imperceptibly in tiny fluid increments. The steadiest of hands.

Deacon didn't stop talking. He laughed about his suddenly stirring memories. He jabbed that Fei hadn't yet learned how to irrigate properly. He said he could tell by the sound. She called him Dick instead of Deacon. The other doctors, the technicians and the nurses all began to chuckle at them.

"Stop making me laugh," Fei said finally. "It's like you're trying to make me screw up. It's your brain, Deacon."

"You've got hands like Lebron James, Fei," Deacon joked. "You could palm my brain like a basketball." Fei watched his eyes close on the giant screen in the corner. He was the most relaxed she'd ever seen him. Why hadn't he been like that before? He just kept joking. "Do you remember the zoo?" he asked. "Stick that little electrode right up near my corpus callosum and get me back there."

Everyone in the room could see Fei's embarrassment. Deacon knew it. "Get your minds out of the gutter, people," he cracked. "All we did was break into a vacant gorilla cage, strip naked and give the onlookers a good lesson in..."

"Deacon!" Fei shouted. Then her thoughts raced. She'd made it seem as though there was something to what he was saying. "I mean... we didn't do anything...not that we didn't do anything..." She went back to her patient omm.

Though they might have laughed a moment before the room was suddenly somber. There were only a few reasons Deacon could reckon why they might be concerned. He cleared his throat and struggled slightly against the tight screws in his skull. "Is it my life or my mind that's on the line?" he asked forcefully.

Fei sighed. "Well, Deacon. That's up to you. Not only is there a growth on the anterior choroidal artery, but it looks like all of the meninges in that area grew at the same pace. They've sandwiched not only the choroidal artery but also the internal carotid artery and they're slowly but surely choking off the oxygen supply to your brain."

All of the doctors looked around for answers but no one seemed to have any. They all just waited for someone, anyone, to make the call.

Deacon pondered the situation himself, tapping his fingers against the table. "We haven't spent all that much time together, but we've shared a lot, Fei." His eyes smiled. "I've actually told you things I've never told anyone else."

A tear ran down Fei's cheek and she laid down her tools.

"I won't remember this so it makes it all the more special. It only lives right here, right now." He too started to cry. "I really believe that."

Deacon thought for a moment about what he might say, about how personal he should get in a room full of people who he'd met a hundred times but who still were strangers. He decided to let it all go. "Do you ever try to remember what your first kiss felt like or your first taste of chocolate ice cream? I can't. I remember loving them but I can't remember the feeling. I was too overwhelmed to create the memory. That's how you are to me. My time with you was too beautiful to remember."

His throat croaked and he gazed off into the distance. "Well," he said. "You've got to cut out the hippocampus to make room for the tumor growth. I can't let you kill me for the sake of my memories."

Fei's head sagged and her heart sank. She had the opportunity. It was right there. If her hands stayed steady enough and if her scalpel just scraped the artery she could slowly but surely remove the tumor. But he was right. It wasn't worth the risk. She had to save his life. She'd sworn an oath.

She stepped back, her hands lifted like a boxers at her shoulders. The nurse patted some gauze under her eyes to dry her tears. "Let's start with electrical stimulation to see which areas are most available for resection. Hopefully we can salvage some structures."

She touched the electrode to a little section of Deacon's hippocampus. His eyes bolted across the screen in front of her like spinning billiard balls. "That's my divorce. It's right there." He sighed. "I was so relieved."

"Relieved?" Fei asked.

He chuckled. "She just wasn't my true love. I kept trying but I couldn't force my feelings."

Fei touched another section. Deacon breathed in a full lung's worth of air. "Blue. No, white. That's a memory, or maybe a thousand. I think I know what it is. Hitting refresh over and over again on Facebook. In a relationship with Stuart Miller. In a relationship with Jimmy Hadon."

She touched one more spot. His eyes lit up. "Pharmacology lecture." The serenity flushed palpably across his face. "Beautiful. A bright yellow sundress and a flower in her hair. Complexion like pure rose water."

Fei blushed.

"I'm not confident in my ability to finish this procedure," she said calmly.

Deacon laughed. "Then come here and hold my hand while they steal away my soul."

She nodded to the assisting surgeon and he stepped up to operate. Fei felt all eyes on her. Like she was that gorilla mating in the zoo. This was the most intimate moment she'd ever shared with anyone and she was surrounded by uncomfortable aqua-colored automatons.

"Does anyone mind if I step out, wash up and sit with the patient?" she asked.

"Let her go," Deacon ordered. "I'm the Chief of Neurosurgery at this hospital for crying out loud. We can have one little break from protocol here, folks."

Fei ran out of the room, washed her hands and face and came back into the room. She sat with Deacon, looking deep into his eyes until the surgery finished and the propofol haze wore off. By the time they'd reached the recovery room he'd forgotten everything.

Fei asked him out for coffee after he recovered. He pointed to his naked ring finger.

Deacon came back every day to linger at the hospital. Fei watched him roam the halls. She never introduced herself again.

• 13 •

Drew Farnsworth came to Columbus, Ohio three years ago with his fiancé Colleen. He works with Green Lane Design as a data center systems designer. He is also currently developing film properties with his brother Gavin, a director, and his writing partner, Anwar Uddin.

MILES TO GO

BY LAURA MOE

yles Bradford stood at a pay phone near the Speedway station off I-295 in Jacksonville Beach and pretended to talk into the receiver. It was late morning, and he anticipated lots of travelers today. April brought snowbirds out of their winter homes to head north, and Myles was hoping to snag one. He watched for Ohio plates and lone travelers as cars stopped at the pumps.

A dented red Ford Explorer from Ohio pulled up with a solitary woman driver. And a Franklin County sticker. Perfect.

Maybe.

She got out, cocked the fuel pump, and shoved it into her gas tank. At first glance she appeared young with her blonde ponytail and trim figure, but as Myles studied her face he could see the woman had deep lines around her eyes and mouth. After the blonde finished pumping her gas, she grabbed her purse from the seat. Myles noticed she did not lock her car. He hung up the phone, chucked his backpack over his shoulder, and approached the vehicle.

The car was a piece of crap, but no one was inside, the doors were unlocked, and the windows open. That worried him, because that meant she probably didn't have air-conditioning. But the back seat was littered with boxes and nylon bags which meant she was traveling somewhere. Myles hoped she was headed for Ohio. There was a chance she was moving here and not headed north, but Myles didn't have time to over-think this. He needed to get to Ohio. He shoved a bag aside and eased himself inside the back. He curled up behind the driver's seat and covered himself with a beach towel from the floor. This used to be easier when he had the limber muscles and tendons of a teenager, not a thirty-year-old. It was warm inside his terry cloth cocoon, and his pack smelled like dirty socks, but he needed it as a pillow.

The driver's side door squeaked as it opened. Myles held his breath. The most dangerous part of flight is during takeoff as the plane thrusts down the runway, builds its momentum and sucks in everything in its path. *If man was meant to fly, he'd have wings,* Myles thought. And if man was meant to hide in the backs of cars, he'd be invisible, not hiding in plain sight in the back of a stranger's car.

The driver tossed something on the passenger seat and opened a can of pop. *Too early for a beer,* he thought. When the blonde driver sat behind the wheel the seat shifted slightly, tightening the corset around his body. Myles wanted to throw the towel off and suck in air, but he waited. The woman fumbled around a bit. He heard the unfolding of a map, and crinkling of pages. The driver muttered something to herself and shut the door. Her seat belt zipped from above his head and she clicked it closed. The ignition buzzed like a bug zapper then engaged. The gears thunked as the woman shifted to D and pulled away from the pump. Miles breathed. The danger was over. For now.

The driver rattled a bag, chips or something. Myles was consoled by the snap and crunch; it meant she had not noticed him. He wished he could sit up and say, "Don't be alarmed, I'm just along for the ride." No chance that would go well.

She reached inside the bag again before it slid between the two front seats. Myles lifted the towel for some air and saw the bag contained pretzels. He hadn't eaten much the last couple of days and those pretzels sure looked good. Maybe he'd get lucky and the bag would tilt and a few would roll his way.

The engine whined and they were on the road. The blonde fiddled with the radio station and stopped at one playing Adele's hit song, "Rolling in the Deep." She sang along, loud and off key, until the music thankfully sputtered out of range. The driver fumbled some more and found another station that played classic country. The driver again sang along when the radio blasted Patsy Cline's, "Crazy." The blonde seemed to only know the first few bars of the song and she mumble-hummed the rest. To drown out her singing, Myles rested his head against the floor board and the steady rhythm of the wheels against highway lulled him into some much needed sleep.

The car stopped and Myles awoke. Why were they stopping already? She couldn't be out of gas.

Shit. Maybe she'd noticed him and pulled over to flag down a patrol car. Plan A: stay put. Plan B: quick exit.

Myles heard her door creak open and her footsteps move away. He held his breath a few seconds and peered through the space between the driver's seat and the headrest. A rest stop. He expelled his breath. It didn't look like they were in Florida anymore. Georgia most likely. He grabbed a fistful of pretzels and quickly chomped them down. He reached for her can of Diet Coke and sucked down the few drops that remained. Myles would have liked to get out and stretch his legs, too, but he crawled back under his towel.

When the blonde came back she tossed her now empty can of Diet Coke in the back and it landed on Myles's hip. She opened another can. He could feel her standing there, looking around her vehicle, perhaps sensing something was off, that animal instinct that senses a predator is near. Then he heard the rattle of the map, and Myles relaxed. She sat back down behind the wheel and pitched the map to the passenger side. She slammed the door and backed the Explorer out. Myles didn't hear her click the seat belt until they were almost back on the freeway.

Myles closed his eyes and listened to the comforting thump thump thump of tires on asphalt. It was the most familiar sound of his childhood, and his earliest memories were like snapshots taken from car windows. When Myles was around five years old, he and his brother Larry sat in the rear of their Ford LTD station wagon. They were moving again. This time from Illinois to New Mexico. As usual, his parents packed the car and left in the middle of the night. Myles slept through Illinois and woke up near the border of Kansas and Oklahoma.

Myles recalled his fascination for the changing landscape, the flat green of Illinois and Missouri bleached into the chalky dust of Oklahoma. "Everything's made of sand," Myles said when they crossed into New Mexico. The sky was also a brighter hue of blue.

His father laughed, and glanced at his wife. "See? I told you the kids would enjoy the change of scenery."

Much later, Myles found out why his family lived on the move, sometimes living in the station wagon. His father had an arrest warrant for armed robbery, and his mother had a habit of passing bad checks. By the time Myles was thirteen, the family had lived in forty-two of the fifty states, including Hawaii. Myles and his brother were educated by PBS from various motel room TVs and thirteen volumes of the 1972 World Book Encyclopedia their mother had bought at a yard sale in Utah.

While they were on the road, Myles's mother kept the family occupied by reading aloud to them. She read Shakespeare's plays, where she feigned an English accent, and she helped the boys memorize poems. "If you have nothing to read, you can entertain yourself by recalling poetry," she had told her boys.

The boys' mother also posed math problems. "If we have fourteen dollars and seventy two cents with fifty miles to go, and gas is a dollar twenty-five a gallon, how far can we get and what can we afford for dinner?"

Their father taught them the indigenous flora and fauna at the innumerable camp sites in each state. Myles learned about weather by living in it. "You're being educated like an Indian," his father told him.

"More horse sense than the nonsense you get in school. You'll be better off, believe me. Your mother and I each suffered twelve years of school and look what good it did us."

The last time Myles visited his mother, she told him her biggest regret was, "that you boys didn't get a proper education."

Myles was sixteen the first time he stowed away. By then both his parents were doing time, and he and his brother lived in separate foster homes in Columbus, Ohio. Larry attended an inner city high school on the near east side, while Myles lived in a northern suburb near the country club.

One day, as he loitered in front of a Seven Eleven after school, Myles noticed a pickup truck for a TV repair service with an address in Larry's neighborhood. He hadn't seen his brother in several weeks. Myles climbed into the back and lay under a tarp. The driver never knew he was there.

A couple of days later Myles crawled into the back of a sedan at a grocery store driven by a careless old woman wearing a bright red wig. Not because he wanted to go anywhere in particular. He just wanted to see how far he could go.

The driver started singing again, this time to the soundtrack of *West Side Story*. When she belted out, "Mariiiiaaaa," it sounded like a cat being strangled. Myles stuck his fingers in his ears and laid his head closer to the side of the car and let the whirr from the tires drown her out. His mother used to sing Beatles tunes and folk songs to them on the road. She had a nice voice. Not recording contract quality, but at least she stayed on key and knew the words to the songs.

As awful as her voice was, this driver wasn't the worst ride Myles had taken. On a seventy degree sunny day, the kind of weather when most drivers roll down their windows, or at least run the AC, this old guy with stooped shoulders and thick lenses drove with the car sealed like a zip-lock bag. As the sun hit the glass, the temperature inside the car quickly rose to above ninety. Myles had hunkered down in the back, sweating under a blanket that reeked of moth balls. The man drove like a snail, and it seemed forever before the old codger turned onto the highway, heading for what Myles hoped was the Cleveland area. He'd had a Cuyahoga County sticker on his license plate.

The Stones were playing at Blossom Arena that weekend, and Myles had a legitimate ticket. No money to get there, though.

At least once every five minutes the old geezer cleared his throat of what sounded like a hairball. In between he whistled off key. The old man had not gone on the freeway; instead, they snaked along on a two lane, curvy road. Every few feet the guy would speed up then slow down. Inside the car the air was thick as sauce, and the irregular motion made Myles's stomach churn. He held his head in his hands and tried to breathe between his fingers, but the car lurched back and forth like a boat lost in the ocean. Myles threw off the blanket, and yelled, "Stop the car, old man."

The old guy swerved and nearly smashed into a tree. "Who…who are you?" he asked. "What the hell are you doing in my car?"

"Just stop the car before I hurl."

The old man pulled off the road. Myles opened the back door and vomited. He leaned out the door and took several deep breaths.

"How did you get in my car?" the man asked.

Myles rested his head against the back seat. "I got in when you were paying for gas."

"Are you planning on robbing or killing me?"

Myles looked at the guy and grinned. The car was a beat up, twenty-year-old Bonneville with ripped seats. The man obviously hadn't bought any new clothes since Nixon was president. "No, man. I just needed a ride."

"You could have hitchhiked. That's how I got around during the war."

"Yeah, I could have," Myles said. He didn't like hitching, though.

He never knew what kind of character might pick him up. This way Myles had some control.

"Well, if you need a ride I can take you as far as Route 13 in Milton Station where my daughter lives," the man said.

"Only if you let me drive," Myles said.

Myles avoided passenger cars temporarily and stuck to flat beds and pickups. He started taking the bus if he had cash, and thumbed rides for a while after he broke his ankle jumping off a moving truck. Its driver had spotted him and yelled he was "gonna kill 'im," so Myles leaped off the back and hobbled into the nearby woods.

Myles spent this past winter in Florida, partly to be near his mom, who was serving time in the Women's Correctional facility in Ocala, and partly because it's easier to live cheaply in a warm climate in winter.

Now Myles was headed back to Ohio to see Larry. This might be the last time. Larry had told Myles on the phone he was full of cancer, "The doc says I don't have much time left. Couple of months. Tops."

Larry offered to send Myles a bus ticket up north, but Myles said, "No, I'll get a ride."

Larry knew all about Myles's transportation system. He tried it himself once, but deemed it too risky. "Jesus, Myles, what if you get arrested?"

"Haven't yet," Myles said.

"What if you don't make it in time?"

"I'll make it," he said. "Don't worry." Myles didn't want to hurry his brother's death.

Myles dozed off, and when he opened his eyes again, it was dark and the driver was slowing down. She stopped and got out of the car. When her footsteps sounded far away, he peered up and read the sign: Bee Line OTEL. Myles would have liked to have stayed in the car all

38

night while she rested in the motel, but he couldn't risk the driver finding him when she came back to get her luggage. He grasped his pack and carefully extended his body over the front seat and got out on the passenger side. He stretched the ache from his legs.

Myles figured it was warm enough that he'd be okay sleeping outside all night. He could get back in the car in the morning when she returned the room key. He paced around outside the rental office, feeling the life come back to his legs. By the time he noticed the No Vacancy sign the driver had come out of the office. She got back into the Explorer and drove away.

Myles sighed, and walked through the parking lot, looking for a car with Ohio plates.

• 13 •

Laura Moe, a self-confessed addict to *The Big Bang Theory* and mocha lattes, spends her weekdays torturing verbs and nouns from her high school English students. She holds an MFA in creative nonfiction, and her work has been published in several journals and anthologies, including the *Cleveland Plain Dealer*, *Brevity, 5AM, Women's Words and Mischief, Caprice* and *Other Poetic Devices*. Follow her on Twitter @LauraMoewriter, and visit her writing blog: laura-moe.blogspot.com/

X I I I

By Rachel Crow

At 11:32 pm on October 27, we met in the parking garage across the street from our apartment. We'd been considering it for weeks, but I never expected to actually go through with it. I'm not, and never have been, a thief.

As we stayed close to the walls, I started picking at the nail polish on my fingers. I forced myself to stop, knowing that Jared would immediately catch it. I knew he'd worry and suggest we go back, but I couldn't do that to him. We needed to do this. The thought of how dire our situation was made me stop for a minute. I never thought we'd end up this desperate.

"Randi, hurry up!"

His aggressive whisper snapped me back into reality. He was halfway up the flight of stairs, while I was standing at the bottom clutching the railing. I ran up the stairs after him. We came up to the third floor, the green level. Seeing how many business workers and apartment dwellers left their cars in overnight parking was like heaven for us. At least it was for Jared. I saw his normally stoic face momentarily light up as his eyes swept over the sea of chrome that lay before us. This is what we had talked about for months. Jared rolled up the sleeves to his black turtleneck as he looked around.

"Well, let's get started."

He made his way over to the car closest to him and got to work picking the lock. I followed slowly, unable to stop myself from looking over my shoulder every ten seconds. I stood off to the side while he worked. I knew that if I tried to help, I would just get in the way. We had already discussed our jobs. He would break in and grab everything, and I would be the one to carry the bags. I couldn't help but admire the grace and speed with which he performed his task. Before I knew it, he was already in the driver's seat, looking around for the most valuable things he could find. I caught a glimpse of my favorite of his tattoos as he handed me a shopping bag from the passenger's seat. The ink was a simple "XIII" on his left wrist. Every time I saw it, I remembered the day he got it.

We were both eighteen at the time, best friends for five years. It was his birthday, and he had been talking for years about getting a tattoo. When he told me about the idea, I was confused. "Why thirteen?" I kept asking him, but he always brushed the question off. When the time came to get his tattoo, I was completely frustrated with him because he had still given me no answer.

The process took a grand total of an hour, including waiting and prepping, and it was the most aggravating hour of my life. Jared didn't say a word the entire time he was being worked on, and the thoughtful look in his eyes never faded. For the entire time I've known him, Jared has never been one to express much emotion. Even that day, the day he had talked about for at least three years, he showed no happiness, pain, apathy, or anything. Just thought.

When he was done, he paid the man, and we left. We decided to get ice cream, and sat on a bench eating, him staring at his wrist the entire time. Finally, I couldn't bear it any longer.

"Jared, please. Why thirteen?" He looked at me with the most amused smile I had ever seen grace his face.

"Why not?"

"Because thirteen's so unlucky!"

"Hm...It is, isn't it?"

41

"Jared, come on! Just tell me!"

"Because, Randi. Life is a game. In the majority of board games, how many dice do you usually roll?"

"Two," I replied, still as confused as I had been for the past few years.

"That's right," he confirmed, "and the highest number you can roll is?"

"Twelve."

"Exactly." We sat there in silence for a moment as I tried to make sense of what he just told me. I looked at him and shook my head.

"I still don't understand."

"I didn't think you would. Twelve is the highest number you can get in a board game. So that means thirteen is impossible to get. It's always just out of reach. That's just like human nature. We always want the highest or the best or the greatest of whatever we can get. What happens when we get the best, or the most recent? What happens when we get the twelve in the game? We always go for what we can't have. We always want what others have, and what's just out of our reach. We want a thirteen."

As he took another bite of his waffle cone, I just looked at him. This boy that I had been friends with for years had stunned me speechless. It was like meeting a whole new person. It took me a few minutes to silently explore the familiar curves of his face, and the beard that grew uniformly and thickly from ear to ear. He glanced at me over his thick-rimmed glasses and just smiled. All I could do was return the smile.

"Randi, let's go. We need to keep moving."

I snapped back into focus again. Without even knowing it, I had been taking items from him and putting them into the bag. He had already closed the first car and was in the driver's seat of the one next to it. I hurried to catch up with him.

"Why are you so distracted tonight?" he asked as he quickly, yet thoroughly, searched through this new car.

"I don't know. It just all seems so ridiculous." He stopped what he was doing and just looked at me.

"What does?"

"Everything! Just...this whole situation, I guess. I saw your wrist and I just started thinking. And now I can't believe we're actually going through with this. Jared...I don't know if I can."

At this, Jared got out of the car and put his hands on my shoulders.

"Randi, you know we have to."

"I know, but..."

"No buts. We need to do this. Do you want to pay the rent?"

"Of course."

"And do you want to someday finally have our wedding?"

"You know I do."

"Then get your mind in the game." With that, he got back in the car and started handing me items once more. I took them without question until I couldn't help myself anymore.

"Jared? What if this is our thirteen?"

Jared stopped what he was doing and just stared at me. The moonlight coming in from the windows of the garage highlighted the dark circles under his eyes, the reminders of the months of sleepless nights that he had suffered through to plan for our future. I knew he had been thinking the same thing, but he never would've voiced it. He never wanted me to worry.

"No. Don't say that. It's not, and you know it," he said as he tried to get back to the car.

"But what if it is? What if we're just not meant to have a nice apartment or a wedding, or even money at all? What if this is just our thirteen, and we're working for something that we can't have?"

"Randi, just stop!"

The intensity of his voice sent a chill down my spine. I watched him as he bent forward and rested his elbows on his knees, cradling his head. He didn't look at me for what felt like an eternity. I hated seeing Jared like that, and even more so because I knew it was my fault. Somewhere off in the distance, I heard the clock chime midnight. He looked up at the last chime, shaking his head.

"I'm sorry," he whispered.

"Don't be. I shouldn't have said it. Come on. Let's finish what we've started."

He stood up and started working, only slightly slower than he had been at first. We finished the second car, and then quickly moved onto the third.

"Hey!"

The shout echoed off the walls, and caught both of us by surprise. We both looked up to see a middle-aged man dressed in a black suit, most likely someone who was pulling extra hours at the office. He stared at us, trying to make sense of what he was seeing.

"What are you doing to my car?"

The realization of the situation hit me like nothing I had ever felt before. I had directly affected this man's life, a man that I had never met and had never done me any wrong. This man probably had a wife, some kids, a nice house, and he clearly had a well-paying job, judging from his suit and the car we were robbing. He looked at us with a look of sheer disbelief, and I didn't blame him. He took a few steps closer to us, demanding an answer just from his body language. Jared grabbed my arm and whispered into my ear.

"Run."

I turned to look at him, and his face was set in its characteristic stubbornness, but there was something else there. His eyes shown with a worry unlike any I had ever seen. I knew what he had said, and I knew what he wanted me to do. The only problem was that I couldn't leave him.

"What?"

"You heard me. You know what I said. Run."

44

"Hey, you kids! Get the hell away from my car!" The man kept taking long steps toward us, gaining momentum in his voice and his stride. Jared pushed me toward the stairwell, shoving the bag into my hand as he did.

"You know what to do," he told me as he went to confront the man. I ran towards the stairs, not once considering that Jared wouldn't make it out of the garage. As I ran, I heard them yelling back and forth, but I didn't know exactly what they were saying. I caught key words like "cops," "accident," and various threatening curses and promises. The last thing I heard before I reached and descended the stairs was Jared yelling to me.

"You're my thirteen! Remember that!"

As I exited the garage, I had no time to think. All I could think to do was to go back to the apartment. Jared's words kept ringing through my head. What did he mean? I was never out of his reach. We had been friends for years, dated for just as long, and had been engaged for the past two years. No matter how hard I thought about his last words to me, I couldn't understand what he meant. I wasn't impossible to get; I was already his. I set the bag down on the couch in our tiny living room, collapsed into the adjacent matching armchair and cried.

What seemed like both an eternity and a fraction of a second later, I heard police sirens going in the direction of the parking garage. I jumped up and ran over to the window that faced the same direction. I couldn't see very clearly because of a tree branch in the way and half of an office building, but I did see the unmistakable red and blue lights coming from the third level. I collapsed to my knees and did what I had not done for years. I prayed. At that moment, there was nothing else I could do. I prayed and cried until I couldn't do either anymore. By the time I opened my eyes again and regained my composure, the lights were gone, and the streets were silent. I was alone in the apartment with nothing but the ticking of the clock and the promise of money from the night's bounty to comfort me.

I lay in my bed trying to force my brain to quiet down long enough to let me sleep, but it didn't work for very long. The sleep that did come to me was filled with sirens and images of the evening's activities. Once three o' clock rolled around, I decided that good sleep was impossible, so I went back out into the living room. I sat next to the bag of loot and stared at it. I couldn't get my brain to wrap itself around one thought or another. As soon as I started focusing on one thing, another thing took over my attention. Sirens, thirteen, tattoos, cars, Jared, everything flashed into my focus and was gone as fast as it came.

Before I knew it, it was 8:00 am. With one last glance out the window at the parking garage, I knew what I had to do. I picked up the bag and headed out to my car. First thing first—I needed to finish out our plan. This bag needed to be empty as soon as I could manage. I went all around the city, pawnshop to pawnshop, selling everything from radios to bags to CDs. By noon, the bag was empty. I sat in my car in the parking lot of the final pawnshop and closed my eyes. My lack of sleep was finally catching up to me. I decided to just rest for a moment before taking the money to the bank.

I woke up with a scream when I heard a knock at my window. With a quick look around, I found that I was still in my car, but the sky was now black and mine was the only car left in the lot. I looked over to see who had disturbed my sleep, and there stood a tall man with an unmistakable police uniform. He motioned for me to roll down the window.

"What're you doing, miss?" he asked, looking suspiciously at me and my passenger's seat.

"Honestly, I'm not entirely sure. I was in the shop around noon, came out to my car, and I guess I just fell asleep." The cop nodded and swept his flashlight toward the passenger's seat and the backseat. He returned it back to my face. I squinted against it, hoping that I had sold everything in the bag. If not, I was in deep trouble.

"Alright, miss. I'll let you go with a warning. Head on out of here as soon as you can. This lot is closed now. You're not allowed to be here."

"Alright. Thank you, sir."

My eyes followed the man as he walked back to his car and drove out of the lot. I took another moment to look out of the window to further survey my environment. The parking lot was empty, street lights were on, and all the shops were closed. A quick glance at my phone told me that it was 10:13 at night. It was a wonder that no one had knocked on my window before then. I started my car and drove out of the lot.

I walked into the apartment and set my purse on the couch. I turned on the lights so that I wouldn't feel so alone.

"Jared, I'm home," I called out of habit. When no answer came, I sighed and sat down on the couch. After my impromptu ten hour nap, I didn't feel tired at all, but I forced my eyes shut.

The next morning, I woke up and slowly walked around our apartment, just to solidify in my mind that Jared really hadn't come home, and he was still out there somewhere. Most likely arrested, but I didn't know that for sure. I didn't want to jump to any conclusions, but I didn't know what else to think. After looking through every square inch of the home, I sat back down on my couch, glancing every now and then towards the parking garage. I decided almost immediately that I needed to go there and search. For what, I didn't know, but I needed answers.

It didn't take long to get back up to the third floor. I surveyed the area, matching it with my memory from two nights before. It took a few moments, because everything looked different in the late morning light. I started walking past the first line of cars, getting re-familiarized with the area, remembering very quickly where the action had taken place. I walked over to the scene of our crime, and, sure enough, the third car was there, in the same exact spot it had been nights before.

I casually started walking past it when I heard footsteps behind me. Thinking it would be very suspicious to stop and stare into the window of this car, I continued walking past it, not entirely sure of my destination. I stopped and pulled out my phone as a distraction, hoping I didn't look too suspicious or attract any attention. As the footsteps approached, I realized it wasn't just one, but two sets of feet. I glanced up and saw two women dressed in business attire, chatting.

"I can't believe it," one was saying.

"Me neither. Our own parking garage. You never think of robberies or arrests happening somewhere you usually feel so safe."

"I know. At least they caught the boy. I feel a little better knowing he's not running amuck."

As they began to pass by me, one of the women glanced over at me. She stopped her friend, and took a few steps toward me. I closed my phone and looked back at her, trying not to look as scared as I felt.

"Can I help you?" I asked.

"I was about to ask you the same thing," she replied. "I've never seen you around here before. Are you new here?"

"New to the city?"

"No, the company. I heard we hired a few new people last week. Are you one of them?"

"Oh, no! I'm just waiting for my date. He's taking me out to lunch today."

"Are you Max's girlfriend?" the woman asked with an excited look on her face. When she saw my blank stare, she calmed down a bit. "I only ask because you're standing by his car." I looked at the silver car. It seemed to be taunting me now that I knew its owner's name. I looked back at the woman with a nervous laugh.

"No, no! I just got the wrong car again. He must be parked on the other side of the garage. That's probably why he's not out here right now! I should go see if I can find where he's parked," I said as I took a few steps toward the other end of the garage.

"Okay, well, be careful. There have been robberies this week, and one boy got arrested a few nights ago. This garage isn't as safe as it used to be. A pretty thing like you should try to head on out as soon as you can," the woman advised me.

"Alright, thank you. Have a nice day!"

The women smiled at me, then continued on their way, laughing and chatting as they walked. As soon as I couldn't see them anymore, I ran out of the garage and back to the apartment. I collapsed into a chair at the kitchen table, trembling as I tried to get a grip on everything that had just happened. I now knew for sure where Jared was. There wasn't anything I could do for him at that point, so I just stared at my hands, picking nail polish off until the early hours of morning.

The few weeks afterward went by without event. On November 18th, I woke up and found a letter from Jared amidst the pile of bills slipped in through our mail slot. I quickly ripped open the envelope and read it.

Dearest Randi,

I'm so sorry for all of this. I know you've been worried, and I know you've probably figured out what happened. You're smart. I probably don't have to tell you that I got arrested that night. I'm sorry it took this long to write, and I'm sorry to have put you through all of this. I'm sorry I didn't call. I used my phone call at the police station to call my mom. Needless to say, that didn't go over well. You know how she is. I would've called you since then, but I was too embarrassed. I let you down. I should've called you, I know, but I couldn't and I still can't. I really hope you're okay. I'll be out in a few months. Please come visit me if you can. Please wait for me. It'll go by fast, I promise. Just remember that I love you.

Stay strong,
Jared

PS – Remember when I said you were my thirteen? It's still true. You're my miracle. I don't want you to ever forget that.

I don't know how long I sat there reading and rereading his letter.

49

I finally knew what he meant that night when I ran out of the garage. I was his miracle. Thirteen, an impossibility in the game of life turned possible. Everything suddenly made sense.

That's why I sit here now in this tattoo parlor, the same one we went to four years ago, getting a matching "XIII" on my wrist. Jared gets out next week. This will be my surprise to him. Now, when people ask either of us what it means, I'll know what to say. It's the impossible made possible. A miracle.

• 13 •

Rachel Crow is a resident of Reynoldsburg, Ohio. As the daughter of two writers, writing has been part of Rachel's life for as long as she can remember. During her senior year of high school, she participated in the Mosaic program, which helped her focus on her writing style through various writing projects and also exposed her to Columbus Creative Cooperative. Rachel is currently a freshman at Ashland University studying Instrumental Music Education.

AT THIRTEEN
BY DEBRA FITCH

In March of 1974, months before local television stations aired President Nixon's "I am not a crook" interview and Howard Alk's *Janis* documentary hit the silver screen, I met the boy with whom I'd share my first kiss. Somewhere amid the political upheaval, waiting in lines three blocks long to buy gasoline, and witnessing first-hand the end of the "free love" era without even realizing it, my initial quasi-intimate moment with a person of the opposite sex came and went like a one-hit-wonder.

While some of the finer details may be a bit sketchy, I know for sure the event that rocked my thirteen-year-old world took place during the first real birthday party I ever attended. By "real" I mean that there were more than three guests, things to do besides pin-the-tail-on-the-donkey, and *boys*. Unlike those dreamy images of The Monkees I had plastered on my bedroom walls, they were actual three-dimensional teen and pre-teen male specimens made of flesh and blood.

Boys represented the mystery my girlfriends and I were determined to solve, with their calm confidence, quirky smiles, and their ever-present posse of pals. Their movements weren't unlike those of a school of fish—when one chose to go downstream, they all would go, one unified mass of testosterone joined at the fins. In retrospect, the boys probably regarded *us* with equal measures of curiosity and repulsion, comparable to our female-ish and limited understanding of them. But this was the year of Steve—the boy who enrolled mid-year and wasn't afraid to make his own splash at our school. The boy who understood art and played guitar and practiced Judaism. The boy no one expected. Within a month, Steve had attained rock star status.

My friend Gabby told me about the new guy she'd seen in her 6th period class who reminded her of Omar Sharif from *Lawrence of Arabia*. I didn't know who she was talking about, but the lilt in her voice meant that it must be someone who was pretty *tough*. In those days, we would say that a boy was "tough" whenever they were exceptionally good looking—and Steve was the toughest.

I met Steve in my eighth period art class. Our teacher went over the materials needed for our project that day—a magazine-photo-and-acrylic-paint collage—and the two of us wound up at the supply cart at the same time. Stacks of *Redbook*, *Popular Mechanics* and *Good Housekeeping* lay opposite the paint-splattered glass jars with up-ended, turpentine-fresh paint brushes. We both reached for the same paint brush. Our fingers touched as we grasped the bristles. Our eyes met; the warming effect of his smile melted away any pretense of self-control. I was convinced that the blush burning its way across my face at that moment would become permanent. I wanted to turn away, *I must get away*, I thought, but something about his eyes held me there. Deep brown. Penetrating. They spoke to me in a language I thought was for me alone.

"It's okay, you can have that one if you want it," Steve said, handing the brush to me. I hadn't noticed that he beat me to it. "But only if you show me your collage when you're finished." He smiled, grabbed the two magazines off the top of the pile, and began to peruse the pages. "*Popular Mechanics?*" he whispered, holding a glossy photo of some engine parts in front of me. "Do you think Mrs. Angstrom fixes cars on the weekends?" he snickered, winked, and then returned to his seat.

It wasn't long before Gabby and all of my friends pronounced their infatuation with Steve. That might be an understatement. They were in love with him—in as much as thirteen-year-olds could be in love—but only a few of his acquaintances were lucky enough to receive the coveted invitations to his bar mitzvah after-party.

"What on earth is a bar mitzvah?" my mother asked the night I brought my invitation home from school. My family attended Baptist services on the few occasions we went to church, so I knew I'd have some explaining to do. I carefully followed along the embossed wording with the tip of my forefinger as my mom held the invitation at arm's length in front of her. It was important to me that she read *everything* before I had the document laminated and framed for hanging on my bedroom wall. "And who is this Steve?"

"Steve is my friend from school, Mom. And a bar mitzvah is, well, you know, when Jewish boys become men—when they turn thirteen," I responded proudly. Using the Encyclopedia Britannica in the library during study hall earlier that day had certainly paid off. "But this invitation is for the after-party, not the ceremony—only his family is going to that."

"Will his parents be at this party?" she asked.

"His mom will be there," I added, trying to appeal to her motherly instinct for additional information, and hopefully painting a picture of a safe party environment. The parental permission gods were smiling down on me that day; not only did she say I could go to the party, but she offered to take me shopping for new clothes *and* a birthday gift for Steve.

The following Saturday, one week before the party, I spun in front of the full length mirror in my bedroom, taking in every possible angle of my new garments: a snug-fitting red t-shirt with a tie-dyed peace sign on the front, low-rise elephant-leg jeans that covered the entirety of my platform shoes and whose waist sat perfectly low on my hips, and a brown, braided leather belt with red beaded fringe that hung almost to my shins when tied in front. I knocked the dangling strips of leather with my knees and proceeded to shimmy and clap to Elton John's "Bennie and the Jets" as though I was auditioning for the Solid Gold Dancers. I was a vision of coolness. I was irresistible. At thirteen, getting new clothes was tantamount to winning an adolescent form of an Oscar. I was rewarded for a talent I already knew existed and wondered why people were only now getting around to appreciating it. Too bad my so-called talent and any shred of self-confidence I possessed never failed to desert me upon leaving the comfort of my room.

Between the new "threads" and my frizzy black mane, I convinced myself that I was Janis Joplin's dark-haired sister. My cousin had turned me on to Janis and Jimi Hendrix a few weeks before, and I felt my taste in music beginning to transform. Sometimes I saw the Pearl when I looked in the mirror, and she would smile back at me. Sometimes I didn't recognize the newly-teenaged reflection at all.

I decided to buy Steve an album for his birthday. His favorite group, The Ohio Players, had just released an album called *Pleasure*, and I was the lucky kid who managed to grab the last copy of the LP available at The Harmony House record shop. I remember Mom scrunching her nose up a little when she eyed the album cover, but when she saw how elated I was with the purchase, she shook her head in that all-right-whatever gesture that meant she wasn't going to say anything about it.

The week before the party dragged on like I was counting down to Christmas. My seventh grade teachers might as well have taught classes in Russian that week because I didn't understand a word they said. I didn't even try. In fact, nothing registered for me except the buzz about Steve's party. And it was everywhere: in the hall by the lockers, in the cafeteria and outside during lunch, and even in the library, though it was reduced to whispers, glances, and a few stifled giggles here and there back in the stacks. The majority of these kids weren't invited to the party, and yet discussion about it pervaded the entire school grounds. I didn't mind. It only served to reiterate the fact that I was one of the elite.

One of the select few. One of the chosen. I possessed the equivalent of Veruca Salt's golden ticket.

At 3:29 Friday afternoon before *the* Saturday of the party, the second hand on the wall clock in my last class of the day seemed to stop one minute before the bell. One minute. One minute left before the weekend. One minute until Friday night. One minute until the night before the party. Come on, come on, COME ON!

Brrrrng! My head and shoulders seemed to spill out of my seat before the rest of my body, and at that moment I came as close to flying as humanly possible. My feet didn't touch the ground until I found my bus parked at the head of the pack—the yellow passenger train twenty cars long—patiently waiting to shuttle us middle school monsters home. I sat in the front seat right behind Karla, the bus driver, and I *never* sat in the front seat. *Why is she stopping to talk to everyone? Why doesn't she yell and make everyone sit down for goodness sakes? Can't she see that I'm in a hurry to get home?*

The next morning I was up promptly at nine—without any parental intervention—and went about my chores as if I'd consumed three bottles of RC Cola. My room was spotless before noon; my new clothes were washed, pressed, and neatly hung over my closet door. After holding six or seven of my favorite necklaces across the front of the tee, I decided not to wear any of them. Why distract from the marvelous peace sign that would be covering my chest?

Steve lived in an apartment complex just behind the middle school parking lot, which was about twenty minutes from home. Since I had limited experience attending parties or any other social function, I was unaware that arriving exactly when the party was supposed to start was not cool. After nagging my mom the entire afternoon about leaving our house on time in order to get to the party at 6:30 sharp, we departed at 6:10 on the dot.

Dressed in my seventies splendor, the gift-wrapped-and-not-so-concealed LP tucked under my arm, I stepped out of the car. Turning back to my mom who confirmed it was now 6:33, and that I should call her when I was ready to come home, I slammed the door behind me, faced the apartment building and stood there—motionless—while I listened to her drive away.

Time slowed to a crawl. I walked in stop-motion to Steve's front door, inhaled, exhaled, and rang the bell. Muffled sounds of movement preceded the click of the dead bolt, and the door swung open to reveal a miniature version of Steve. The perfect dimple in this little man's chin grew as a toothy smile spread across his face like an eclipse. It was clear that Jeff, Steve's little brother, possessed charms beyond his age when he gently took my hand, led me through the living room where his mom was watching television, and across the kitchen. The basement door was removed from its hinges and the open doorway beckoned me. I looked back at Jeff who tipped his chin in the direction of the music. The sound ascended the steps before me, encircled my body, urged me down the first step, gripped my arms, and coaxed me into the dimly lit basement. The space was unfinished and sparsely furnished, with bare concrete floors and two shag rugs that glowed neon green under the black light fixtures hanging at either end of the room. Reflective posters with sparkling stars and glowing moons flanked the stairwell; an enormous pink peace sign covered one of the walls. Lavender incense created a thin layer of haze near the back of the room.

I continued to grip the handrail even though I'd made it to the last step. Steve appeared at my right; his beautiful smile—I now recognized it as a larger version of Jeff's—caused my body to stiffen and filled me with a friendly warmth at the same time.

"Deb, you made it!" he said. "Welcome to my birthday bash." He took my hand and I floated along as he guided me through the semi-darkness to a table loaded with food. A 20-gallon cooler filled with lemonade rounded out the offerings.

I gradually recognized my friends Gabby, Sandy, Sherry, Tracy and of course Donna who had called me earlier that day to ask what I was wearing. I guess everyone arrived fashionably early! Besides Steve, there was Joe from my math class, John, Mark, Paul and Scott from my English class—together we formed a perfect dozen. Steve placed his hand on my back and I turned to face him. He calmly pried the tell-tale gift from under my arm and carried it upstairs, taking two steps at a time, and then disappeared.

Meanwhile, I joined the conversation in which Joe, Gabby and Donna were discussing the inner-workings of Steve's bar mitzvah earlier that afternoon. Since they weren't invited to the ceremony either, the entire content of the discussion was conjecture.

"Do you know what goes on during those things anyway?" Joe asked, looking at the three of us as if it were a rhetorical question. "I heard that they have to wear some kind of long silk robe and have to memorize a bunch of stuff to say to a priest."

"You mean a *rabbi*," Gabby interrupted, "and they do have to memorize some stuff."

"Do they have to keep bottles of holy water with them?" asked Donna, her eyes darting between Gabby and me as if she couldn't believe she had let the question slip out.

"No, holy water is used in Catholic churches. My grandparents took us to Mass once on Christmas Eve," Gabby explained. Looking back, I suppose none of us were especially church-savvy.

As it turned out, I was naïve to a greater degree than my friends were about more than just religious practices. In the days following the party, I learned that during the course of that *one* day—his birthday—Steve had "gone with" *and* broken up with three girls. *Three.* I also learned that one of the three girls was Gabby. I suppose it was a case of bad timing; Gabby had gotten upset at Steve for some reason earlier that day, so she broke up with him when she got to the party. *Nice birthday present*, I thought.

When Steve rejoined our group, Gabby and Joe made a beeline for the food table, which left us alone for a moment. Just as Steve began to say something to me, Sherry, the boy-master-manipulator of our group, materialized out of nowhere, strode over to where we stood and wedged herself strategically between us. Steve's eyes followed mine, but Sherry brought her hand to his cheek and turned his head so that he was facing her. She placed her other hand around his waist and held onto the belt loop that was in the middle of his lower back with her index finger.

I found a small hassock positioned under the stairwell, so I had a seat and watched as Joe commandeered the stereo system. Parliament's "Tear the Roof off the Sucker" was the perfect choice to get everyone dancing. As shy as the majority of my friends were, and I was right there among them, music seemed to quell our inner fears and allowed us to be ourselves. All four corners of the room danced with tinted lights that focused up to the ceiling, creating a stream of color that ran from the floor along each of the walls. Joe turned out the lights completely except for the four corners and the two black light fixtures that illuminated the posters, rugs, and our clothing with blazing neon. Once our eyes acclimated to the darkness, it was easy to spot my friends as they danced, walked to the food table, plopped down on bean bag chairs, sat in folding chairs, or relaxed on the two sofas facing each other under the glow of the peace sign.

By the time the first side of the album finished, I had danced and talked to everyone except Gabby. She had switched gears to 'recluse' mode and had taken up residence alongside the lemonade cooler. I'm sure she wasn't too happy about the whole situation with Steve at this point, and Sherry was not shy in her attempts to keep Steve's attention focused on her. But he *had* looked at me when the lights went out.

Just as fast as Joe had turned the lights out, he turned them on again.

"All right everyone, Steve's getting the Coke bottle, so you all know what that means, right?" Joe announced, seemingly pleased with himself for having become the master of ceremonies.

One of the sofas and the coffee table were pushed out of the way and the shag rug beneath it was moved along the wall. The twelve of us sat around the newly cleared space on the floor in a rough circle—six of us managed to get a front seat with the remaining six wedged between us. We crossed our legs so that the gaps between our sets of knees served as the dividing line for bottle-spinning purposes. Joe insisted that Steve, being the birthday boy, would spin first.

He grasped the bottle with his right hand, thumb on one side, his four fingers on the other, and performed a textbook rotation. The bottle spun in place so fast the label in the middle became a blur. *How long had he been practicing that?* I wondered. The glass on the cement floor made a slight clanking sound as it completed its circuits, slowing gradually with each revolution until the last three whump whump whumps before it decelerated. The bottle gently edged its way around to Sandy, then Joe, then Donna, then...Sherry. Our eyes barely had time to register the spin results when Sherry rose up on her knees, leaned across the floor over the bottle area, grabbed the back of Steve's head, shoved her face into his, and planted an audible kiss on his surprised mouth. It lasted a few seconds longer than everyone thought it should—and while a few of us were uneasy, a whistling and cat-calling crescendo emerged from others.

After releasing Steve from her clutches, Sherry spun the bottle but it slowed quickly and everyone stopped breathing until the glass pointed out her next victim—Sandy!

"Hah! Well, that one doesn't count!" Sherry laughed, and grabbed the bottle for spin number two. This time she flipped her wrist with authority, and the bottle spun wildly and wobbled a bit—Joe and Gabby had to shift their legs to get out of the way. The bottle settled right in front of Joe, who systematically, and devoid of any emotion whatsoever, leaned in toward Sherry, pecked her lips, and pushed her shoulders down so that she immediately sat back in place. Several of us looked at each other with stifled laughs, but Sherry, undeterred, continued to wear her Grinch-ish grin.

I found myself looking into the eyes of my friends—smiling along with them, laughing with each spin, with each kiss, and wishing. Wishing Steve's spin would stop at me, and then hoping it didn't. Worrying about it became a moot point; as it turned out, the bottle didn't point to me during the entire course of the game. In a way, I was relieved and in another, I was visibly disappointed in spite of trying my best to hide it. To this day I don't know whether Steve sensed this and decided to improvise rules for a new game; no one else seemed to notice my lack of lip time. I'd never kissed anyone before, and I certainly didn't want my closest friends to see me squirm with nervousness in front of everyone—or worse yet, get laughed at for the effort.

"Okay, enough of that," Steve said, grabbing the bottle and standing up, waving it over his head like one of those men in the orange vests who direct commercial jets into their airport parking spaces. "Let's turn out the lights so that we can kiss whoever we want."

I heard a "far out" escape Scott's lips. Mark and Paul high-fived, Sherry and Gabby went straight toward opposite ends of the room while Donna and Tracy sought out the peace wall and sat on the displaced sofa. Neon fragmented the shadowy room. I could easily see figures, but it was impossible to be certain of anyone's identity unless they spoke or brushed against me. I shuffled my feet across the floor, up and over the second rug so that I wouldn't trip, and then found my hassock under the stairwell where I felt safe.

People were moving from wall to wall and corner to corner—some silhouettes were two bodies across but I couldn't be sure who was who. The soft sounds of kisses, hushed laughter, and scuffling shoes filled the space, their echoes culminating in a single feathery touch that brought gooseflesh to my arms. I closed my eyes for a moment, inhaled the lavender haze, and planted my chin in the center of both palms, elbows resting on my knees. Anxiety rose and, with gentle hands, slowly began to squeeze my throat.

With an indescribable sixth sense, I knew that Steve was there. I felt his eyes looking at me through the dark before I could make out his form. With a searching gesture, his arms found me; his fingers extended until they met mine. With both my hands firmly in his, he pulled me up and toward him. Gently placing my arms around his neck, he reached for my waist and clasped his fingers together at the small of my back. I'm not sure whether it was because I thought I might pass out otherwise, but I laid my head down on his right shoulder—I had no idea what I was doing. *Is this right? What should I do?* We stood there for a moment, breathing in the incense, my Sweet Honesty cologne, and his fresh-shirt-smell. *Do all boys smell this good?* I kept my eyes closed, reeling it all in, and I wanted that moment to somehow freeze and never move forward. His fingers unclasped and the next thing I felt was my face being gently cupped between his hands. Strong hands. When I opened my eyes, his nose was so close to mine that I could feel the softness of his skin even though we weren't really touching. *Were we touching?* I instinctively flinched—ever so slightly—and he carefully pulled me back to him.

"I've wanted to do this since art class," he whispered, his satiny voice caressing me along with his gentle fingertips. Slowly his hands found their way to the back of my neck and gingerly brought my face in close—so close that our breathing became intermingled and I couldn't tell his breath from mine. And then in one sweet, sensuous moment, our lips met.

As if my body knew more about what to do than I did, I found my hands moving through his hair, and I lightly caressed his cheek and chin. In truth, I believe there were actually three kisses, one right after the other, the last culminating in a whisper-delicate brush of his lips across mine.

As our eyes opened, and as if on cue, Joe flipped the light switch and announced he was taking stereo requests. In a moment of temporary blindness, Steve and I separated and reality, along with our vision, found its way back to us. After calling my mom for a ride home, I chatted with Sandy but I don't recall anything that was said. All around me, the sights and sounds merged; I became engulfed within a sort of hazy, mental fog. Pink Floyd's "Us and Them" took me through the last dregs of my lemonade, and the final moments of the evening wound down.

Within a couple of weeks following the party, Steve asked me to *go with* him, and I accepted. It would seem that I was the next female on the rotation. Unfortunately, we never saw each other for the duration of our short-lived relationship. There were many phone conversations, many dramas, but ultimately we parted ways. We didn't speak to each other in art class after the party; it was as if we both decided it was better to pretend that we'd never met. Even though I hoped we might, we never saw each other again after that year of school was over. I later learned that his test scores allowed him to skip a grade, so he graduated one year ahead of us all. As quickly as that, our one-hit-wonder had peaked, and then it fell off the charts without an encore.

* * *

My sister called last weekend to ask if I wanted to go shopping with her and my niece, Kayleigh, who turned thirteen last January. Apparently Kayleigh was looking for something extra-special to wear to her best friend's thirteenth birthday party next Friday night. Between the three of us, we stripped the clothes racks, waded through most of the stores, and dragged multiple shopping bags behind us. Kayleigh got her ears pierced at the corner jewelry store, and beamed while showing us her new pearl studs. *Pearls.*

"Well, a boy in her math class is going to be there Friday night," my sister whispered to me while we waited for my niece to finish trying on a pair of jeans. She winked and pointed her forehead in the direction of Kayleigh's dressing room. "And not just *any* boy."

"Ah, one of *those*," I said. *One of those*, I thought.

After watching my sister and Kayleigh drive away from me through the Indian Mound Mall parking lot, I got into my car and started the engine. *I can't believe she's thirteen already*, I thought. I shut my eyes for just a second, a fleeting attempt to understand the blur that was the last three decades.

I pushed the gear shift into drive, and soon reflections of the traffic lights on Route 79 were sliding green then red across the windshield. The satellite radio started its search program for my favorite artists, but I'd pressed the mute button earlier to answer a cell phone call. An introspective hush filled the cabin of my car.

I turned north on Route 13 toward Utica, and drove a mile or two before I decided to break the silence. The pale blue Sirius Radio ticker lit up the dash with the artist's name—Elton John—and instinctively, I knew. Even before the song title appeared, I knew. Without hesitating, I turned up the volume, opened all the windows, and belted out the most heart-felt rendition of "Bennie and the Jets" ever.

· 13 ·

Debra Fitch is originally from Columbus. She is a full-time student at The Ohio State University where she is majoring in English with a focus in creative writing. She is an avid fan of young adult and speculative fiction, often giving up hours of precious sleep to finish a great book. She supplements her income by doing freelance portrait, wedding and commercial photography. Contact Debra at debra.fitch@yahoo.com, or look for her on Facebook, LinkedIn and Goodreads. You can also follow her book reviews and other ramblings (@d_fitch) on Twitter.

THE POCKET WATCH

BY TODD METCALF

I had exactly one hour to live, and I didn't see any way out. The wind was nonexistent, not even a zephyr brushed my face. Sounds were suppressed inside an invisible vacuum of silence. No one stirred, no people, no animals; everything was tranquil and unmoving as though I were walking through a diorama of the most realistic models ever created.

Everything stopped in the Still Period when I held the pocket watch. Even Time obeyed, especially Time because Time always wins.

That exquisitely detailed gold pocket watch with the most wonderful symbols on its casing controlled Time. An old lady sold it to me at her husband's estate sale. He had passed away twenty years prior, and she finally decided that it was time to sell his possessions and move on. When I came across the watch, it was blackened from years of nonuse and looked like a decrepit relic that could no longer compete in its own race against Time.

As a mechanical engineer who designed mundane wiring assemblies for GM, I was intrigued by tiny and elaborate mechanisms. The inner workings of watches had a beauty and grace of movement that was incomparable. Even if the watch no longer functioned, I could still tinker with it, appreciate its intricate design. I rubbed its blackness and wiped away the smudges of Time. It revealed fantastic engravings of stars and planets and seemed to embody the universe itself.

I pressed the button, popping the lid open. Despite its fancy exterior, the watch's face was nondescript. Numbers were printed in a basic serif typeset. My gaze flowed around the dial, admiring the simplicity of each digit, one through twelve. I closed the case, only then realizing the error. I nearly dropped the pocket watch in my rush to open it again. There was no number twelve on the dial. Instead, thirteen reigned at the top.

I couldn't imagine a watchmaker being so inept. Watchmakers spend thousands of hours crafting each piece individually and fitting the movements lovingly inside its casing. Surely a mistake on the face would be replaced after investing so much effort into the watch's creation. No master would allow that anomaly to stand.

I stared at it, instantly beguiled. It was a gorgeous case with a mystery inside; I had to have it. I was prepared to pay hundreds of dollars to cure my sudden infatuation.

"How much?" I asked the lady.

I had seen her freely smile to previous customers, but when she saw the filthy timepiece in my palm, she wiped the grin from her face.

"Harold loved that pocket watch," she said and then stared at it for a long while. "His distant uncle from the Black Forest made it, but then died as a young man only thirteen days later."

The watch seemed to take on additional heft in my hand. "It's an extraordinary piece."

She nodded. "Harold cherished that watch. It was his favorite possession." She sighed, lost in the tide of memories.

"I can see why he liked it. The engravings are amazing."

"He owned it less than two weeks. Thirteen days, actually."

"That's unfortunate," I said. "I'm sorry."

"He died with it in his hand."

I nearly dropped it even though I knew I was being foolish. For some reason, the last object that a person touches upon death retains the most meaning, as though the person's essence were transferred into it.

"I'm sorry. Perhaps you should keep it." I handed it to her even though I desired it more than anything I had ever wanted in my life. I felt an almost supernatural attachment to it, but I knew I could never take something from her that meant so much.

She waved her hands adamantly but was careful not to touch it. "I don't want it."

I understood. It held too many memories and keeping it would remind her of all that she had missed in the last twenty years.

She studied me and then seemed to decide that I had come to the wrong conclusion. "I'm not sure you should have it, either. I'm not sure anyone should have it."

I nodded, realizing how no one could appreciate its sentimental intensity. "I'll take care of it as though it were my own father's."

"It's not that," she said. "I should destroy it, but I'm afraid of the repercussions."

I wasn't sure what she meant. I didn't care. I would do anything to have it. "It's a work of art. It would be a terrible loss to the world if you destroy it."

"Maybe I should keep it..."

"Please, this is the most wonderful pocket watch I've ever seen. What can I give you for it?"

"It's special. No amount of money would be enough."

I couldn't tell if she was being shrewd or delirious. I pulled out my wallet. I took out the wad of bills and counted them. "I only have eighty-seven dollars and..." I searched my pockets. "Forty-three cents." I presented them to her, but she stared at the watch in my other hand.

"I'll come back and give you more if you want. Please. I'll treat it like a priceless gem."

She sighed, long and hard. "Be careful," she said as she took the money.

I thanked her profusely and sped home to clean it and find an answer to the mysterious thirteen.

Once the filth was polished away, the gold case sparkled, revealing detail that could only be created by a master craftsman. I searched for an answer to the mystery, but it was too complex for Google and the limited data I had to go on. I would have asked the lady about its history, but I figured that the more I probed, the more likely she was to keep it.

I disassembled it and spread its contents on the kitchen table because the overhead chandelier offered the best light. Over the next several days, I raced home from the office and spent the entire evening exploring its inner workings and repairing what I could make out. The complexity was astounding. The more I learned about it, the more I realized that I would never completely understand its grandeur. Yet each night, it seemed to hold fewer of its secrets. Parts just fit together. Gears rotated freely. It was almost as if it were fixing itself. I chalked it up to the fact that my subconscious mind had finally grasped its design.

After seven days, I sealed the back of the case and rotated the hands to 11:29. Then I wound it. I held my breath.

The second hand ticked forward. When it passed the number thirteen, the minute hand moved one tick mark. I listened to the steady tick-tick-tick as though it were a symphony. I stared at the hands of Time turning in my palm. I placed it on my nightstand and fell asleep as it watched over me.

In the morning, I awoke one hour earlier than normal, feeling amazingly refreshed as though I had slept the entire seven hours. After I completed my normal morning routine, I slid my new treasure into my pocket and went for an uncharacteristic stroll before work.

The morning proceeded normally after that, although I grew hungry before my noon visit to Dan's Deli down the street. At 11:40, I could ignore my hunger no longer and found myself ordering the usual pastrami on rye from Lorraine.

"You're here early," Lorraine said. "I don't think I've ever seen you here before 12:05 in the last three years I've worked here."

"I had a great night's sleep and woke an hour early. My stomach didn't get the message."

"Well, make the most of your extra hour. It's not often we're given a free one."

I sat at the long table that lined the front windows. The window seat gave me a good perch to people-watch.

When I had taken the final bite of my sandwich, the world stopped.

It was as though someone had hit the pause button on the planet. The man walking on the sidewalk in front of me froze in mid-step. Cars became immediately stationary. They didn't brake to a stop. There was no squealing of tires, no drivers thrusting forward against their seatbelts, no deploying of airbags. A woman's silk skirt that had been dancing in the wind now defied gravity, its pleats petrified in an outstretched wave. A burly man sitting next to me held a steaming cup of coffee against his lips, the waft of steam immobile, like a stalagmite rising out of the black liquid. Lorraine stood motionless behind the counter, her face caught in the middle of a blink, like a reunion picture taken from the clueless aunt who always crops her subjects out of the frame or catches them with their eyes half-closed.

I cautiously reached over to touch the man sitting next to me. He felt like iron. It wasn't just his large, firm bicep that was solid, but his polo was hard like titanium. He was essentially a statue, a breathless effigy formed with lifelike flesh and clothing. I pushed him, but he didn't budge.

Everyone in the deli and on the street had instantly become static and fossilized. I pushed the deli's door and smacked my face against its resistance. I checked the lock then looked for another source of impedance. I braced my shoulder against it and thrust. It eventually gave way by inches.

Outside, the sounds, or the lack of them, struck me at once. I approached the lady with the splayed skirt despite the absence of a breeze. I waved my hand in front of her face. She didn't blink. I screamed in her ear. It had the same effect as shouting at a skyscraper.

I ran. I halfway expected the other streets to be normal, as sometimes happens when the electricity goes out on one street but remains working on the next. But it wasn't meant to be. The entire world had solidified.

Fighting panic, I jogged for what seemed like hours. When my lungs could no longer keep up, I gasped for breath, loathing the world of immobility and lifelessness. Anger slowly replaced my panic. I approached a man frozen in the middle of a conversation on his cell phone. I kicked him hard in the chest. As he wobbled, I pushed him over. He clanked against the sidewalk like a cheap statue. A woman nearby hovered above the ground in half-stride. Placing my hand on her rigid shoulder and using my full weight, I pulled her to the ground. The things that normally moved had become instantly obdurate. They were capable of movement, except that they resisted it with the stubborn will of Time.

Being surrounded by people who could neither move nor talk was nearly indescribable. I was a hairsbreadth away from insanity. I ran and shouted and pushed and ultimately crumpled onto the ground, crying for evidence of life in a barren world. Imagining a life in this abomination of Time was unthinkable.

In the stillness of my silent world, the pocket watch ticked. Before I could pull it out of my pocket, I was back at Dan's Deli sitting in the same seat I had taken nearly an eternity ago. Sounds flooded the world in a deafening roar. The burly man on my left sipped his steaming cup of coffee and set it down. Outside, the woman's skirt wafted freely in the breeze. The door of the deli slammed shut.

I dashed outside to greet the bustle of life. People walked and talked, cars sped along, activity was everywhere. I ran to the next street. The jogger I had pulled to the ground brushed her sweatpants as she tried to explain to a passerby how she had fallen with no memory of doing so. The man on the cell phone that I had kicked now clung to his chest like he was having a heart attack.

I pulled out the pocket watch to see that it was only two minutes past thirteen. Time had stopped around me. How was it possible? I wondered, shuddering at the answer too outlandish to admit. This peculiar little watch, with the thirteen instead of a twelve, had stopped Time.

I don't recall what happened the rest of the day. I returned to work and shifted some paper around on my desk and deleted email messages without really reading or replying to them. At home, I continued my usual routine except that instead of preparing for bed at 10:30, I waited. I waited for midnight because thirteen was the pocket watch's magic number. Either that or it would be the bewitching hour of my insanity.

Since everything had stopped at noon, I thought my electric lights wouldn't work so I would need a light source to see. I lit a series of Yankee Candle tapers that my mom had given me on my last birthday. I flipped the cover on the watch open for the umpteenth time. One minute to thirteen. I waited as the seconds ticked, each mark like a gunshot to my ears. When the minute hand reached thirteen, the watch stopped. Silence filled the room. The din of traffic outside my apartment ceased. The candles stopped flickering, but their light still reached my eyes. I knew enough about physics to know that if time stopped, then light should too and my vision would be nonexistent. Somehow it didn't work that way.

I pulled my apartment door open, then the door to the steps, then the one at the bottom. I forced the front door of my apartment complex open and staggered into the motionless street. Everything was still, as it had been at noon earlier in the day.

I concentrated on tracking the passage of time in my head. After what seemed like an hour, I found myself transported back to my kitchen table holding the watch, the candles flickered their appreciation. The sounds of nighttime resumed, and the world continued on its way as though nothing peculiar had ever happened.

I finally understood the special power of the watch. Every twelve hours when the minute hand touched thirteen, the world would stop for one hour. I considered the implications. Every twelve hours I would get one free hour that no one else had. Every day I'd have two free hours when everyone else was limited to twenty-four. It was like changing from daylight saving time twice every day. I jumped back two hours a day.

Over the next several days, I started looking forward to the Still Period. The lack of sound remained unsettling but not so unnerving that I couldn't be productive. I experimented with the random hour I was allotted every twelve hours. When the world was Still, I learned I could influence things on a limited basis, but I was prevented from making meaningful changes because Time resisted change. I couldn't travel far because cars didn't work, and I always returned to the same place I had been no matter how far away I walked.

I started planning activities in my extra two hours. I routinely left one hour earlier from work because I completed an hour's worth of work during the Still Period at noon. That gave me two hours in the evening. In those additional two hours, I could accomplish much more than a mere mortal with only twenty-four.

Imagine, two hours more than everyone else on the planet. I had never had an advantage in my life. I was a solid B student in high school and college, a consistent performer at work, but I was never considered a leader or someone who would make a large contribution to society. But the pocket watch would change all that. I was the only person who had the gift of Time.

By the second week, the watch had changed me. I became a new person. My attitude improved. Instead of being pushed along by life, I owned it. I became productive. Women appreciated my new air of confidence. The upper executives in my company started taking notice.

On the thirteenth day since I had gotten the pocket watch to work, I awoke and excitedly consulted my list. After nearly thirty years of mediocrity, my life had just started to begin. I jumped out of bed and arrived at work as quickly as I could. I dove into my tasks and nearly forgot to take time for lunch.

As I stood on the street corner, I consulted my watch. It was nearly thirteen. I realized that I wouldn't make it to Dan's Deli before the Still Period. I had to eat my sandwich before everything stopped, otherwise the food would turn into an inedible chunk of petrified solid. I would have to go hungry for one more hour.

It was only three seconds before the minute hand touched thirteen when I heard a car engine rev up, off to my left. A woman screamed as a Dodge truck barreled recklessly through the traffic. It jumped the curb and flew directly at me. I cowered. The truck stopped in midair an inch from my face.

I was in the Still Period. That meant that no matter what I did within the next hour, I would ultimately return to this spot, and the truck would end my life.

The old lady had said that her husband's uncle died at an early age, just after creating the timepiece. Her husband died thirteen days after he gained ownership of the watch. I knew that the watch had been responsible for both deaths. Today was my thirteenth day.

I closed the cover on the watch. For the first time I noticed a tortured face, previously hidden in the immaculate engravings on the watch case.

Time was not just stubborn, it was rigid and heartless. Time made sure that everything decays and ultimately dies. Time always wins.

I wrote my goodbyes to those I loved, although frankly very few people cared about me. I had not made much of my life. I had not made many friends, I had not loved, and, worst of all, I had not lived. I thought about the years that I had wasted and about the years that I would no longer have. The pocket watch had given me a moment to consider how I had squandered a life full of potential.

I opened the case and gazed at the peculiar face with no twelve. The additional hour the pocket watch freely offered its owner was a curse, especially on the thirteenth day when it called in its chit. I was determined that no one would fall under its evil spell again. No one else would ever own it.

I placed it on the sidewalk and lugged a loose brick from the crumbling wall surrounding a parking lot. I didn't know what the pocket watch would do. It may condemn me to wander the Still Period forever, or it may force me to meet the grill of an oncoming truck.

I didn't care. I would make my life matter.

I hefted the brick over my head and brought it down, flattening the watch with a satisfying thud. I squeezed my eyes closed, preparing for my fate.

Nothing happened. I gazed at the stillness surrounding me. When I considered the loneliness, I realized that it had punished me for my insolence.

I gathered the broken pocket watch in my hand and stared at the number thirteen on its face. In its last gasp for life, the pocket watch ticked.

• 13 •

Todd Metcalf was born and raised in Columbus, Ohio, and attended New Albany High School and The Ohio State University. After graduation, he worked in various technology and executive management positions with some of Columbus's top companies. He currently runs a business consulting company serving the vibrant business community in central Ohio. He is happily married with two wonderful daughters.

THE HANGMAN'S CRAFT

BY AARON BEHR

Earnest Lauder sits quietly across from Professor Reichmann. He is quiet, emotionless, and patient. Reichmann, a forty-year-old kindly-looking bald man, returns the same countenance. This is the first time Earnest has encountered someone so educated. Normally these types of killers are uneducated. They are intelligent, just not so eloquent. Their passion is direct and wild.

"You have my weight? Two hundred and twenty pounds. My height is five feet ten inches." Professor Reichmann shoves his glasses higher on his face. "There is not much more that you need."

They stare at each other. The gray prison visiting room binds them into the same shallow place. It smells like a fresh coat of paint. The cold room is brightened by a giant barred window. Shadows cast on Reichmann's face add to the feeling of intimidation which Earnest tries not to show. "You know why I'm here?"

"You are a hangman." Reichmann is precise with his vowels. "You are essentially my executioner." He folds his hands and legs. "I find it intriguing that you would want to meet with your...victim... beforehand."

"You're not a victim."

"I'm not?" Reichmann narrows his vision and focuses in on Earnest's eyes. "That's interesting." There is a pause. Reichmann nods then continues, "So tell me. Do you tie a traditional hangman's noose?"

"You're mighty interested in my profession Mr. Reichmann. Why don't I ask the questions?"

"If you insist." Reichmann's grin is friendly, warm, and kind.

"You're a professor?"

"Of world religions and literature. It's a small school so I've had to fill a number of roles. Did you go to college Mr. Lauder?" Reichmann fishes with a question. "Is it okay that I call you Mister?"

Earnest hesitates then replies, "Earnest. You can call me Earnest."

"Very good." There is an uneasy pleasure glimmering in Reichmann's eyes. The sun seems to tease it.

Earnest tries to deflect attention. "So you've done a lot of reading in your day?"

"I have."

"Have you ever read the poem 'Thirteen Turns'?"

"I have not." Reichmann leans in, apparently earnest to hear. "Tell me it."

Earnest scratches his head. "First, tell me why you are in the situation you are in." This ritual is what makes Earnest Lauder the best executioner. Where most stop at stats such as weight and height, Earnest only begins. He believes he has to talk to the man, size him up, and make sure all factors are taken into account. What if the man is prone to tense up or relax? Is he ready to die or fighting it?

"You've read the reports." Reichmann is clearly not happy with the subject.

"I did. Four girls." Earnest folds his hands and locks eyes with Reichmann. "Rape and murder."

"They were teenagers."

"They were children."

Reichmann smiles, removes his glasses, cleans the lenses, and continues, "I'm not going to argue ethical semantics. Less than a hundred years ago girls were being married off at age twelve. There wasn't anything wrong with it then."

"The law today says they were girls, too young to be consensual. Your logic may be golden. I don't give a damn. The law's the law."

"That's where one finds the delight, isn't it though?" Reichmann returns the frames to his head. "You use the word 'consenting' but I'm glad they weren't. Where is the thrill in consensual sex? No matter the age, that one little word transforms it into a crime, doesn't it?"

"Yes sir." Earnest tries to remain placid in his responses.

Reichmann is fishing for something, a trigger, a button, something to shake Earnest. "The first, I smashed her head into the ground. The second, I stabbed. There was way too much blood for my tastes. The third, I managed to break her neck and the fourth, I choked with my bare hands." He pauses to look at his hands. "That was probably the worst. It was slow, too slow. I had too much time to reconsider what I was doing."

Earnest shifts in his chair. He has seen a man choked to death by a hangman's noose. It was a different executioner, not Earnest, who used a seven turn noose. There wasn't enough friction to stop the eye from tightening and break the neck. It should have decapitated the man but he was a wrestler. In his drive to live he tensed his neck. That was the day Earnest swore every neck would break. That was the day he read "Thirteen Turns."

"All in all though," Reichmann continues, "I loved every minute of it."

No remorse. About half of the death row inmates plead innocence or for a reclaimed innocence. The other half live for the wrongs they've committed. They are the ones who don't want to die and are the trickiest to hang.

"I answered your questions. Please...please humor me and answer my own. Will you use a traditional thirteen turn noose?"

"I will."

"I'm guessing that's what your little poem is about?"

"It is."

"Recite it to me. I always love to hear good poetry." Reichmann intertwines his fingers and locks them together. They rest on his stomach.

Earnest is surprised how casually Reichmann moves from savage murder to another topic. "Do you feel any remorse?"

"Not a bit." The words fall flat from Reichmann's mouth.

The chair screams as Earnest scoots it back. "You'd do it again if you could?"

"In a heartbeat." A smile takes hold of Reichmann's face. It's not sinister or evil. It's sad, a smile of mourning. There is a desire to live in his eyes. He desperately clings to life. There is a lover's romance about how Reichmann recalls what he did. It was his passion.

When Reichmann falls, he will tense up. If Earnest didn't know why this man looked so troubled, he would be moved to sympathy by that smile, by the warm friendly look about the man. That is all Earnest needs to finish calculating the drop and satisfy his conscience. Reichmann deserves the noose and it's hard to hide that belief as he says, "Thank you for your time."

"My pleasure." Reichmann sighs, leans back, lifts his locked hands higher on his stomach, and stares at the ground. Space, a far off place, takes hold of his gaze as he dreams.

The sturdy metal door unlocks and begins to swing open.

"Earnest." Reichmann eagerly asks, "Do you know that they call you the last professional hangman?"

Speaking into the door, he replies, "I do." It's not a title he is exactly proud of but one he hasn't tried to dissuade. New forms of execution continue to put Earnest out of work. He doesn't entirely mind that either. "Reichmann, why did you choose to be hanged?"

"I guess it's a sentiment for the old ways of doing things."

There is a pause. Earnest turns his head to the large window. A fenced-in courtyard in front of a great open field forms the picturesque view.

"One last thing." The squeal of Reichmann shifting in his chair reverberates through the bright gray room. "The poem, please indulge me."

Earnest returns to the metal door and replies,

> "Thirteen turns to break a sinner's neck.
> Neck waged and lost by, to death.
> Death, the horseman, patiently waits
> Weights on Justice's scales to speak.
> Speak of sin, of death, and of pride.
>
> Pride moves the sinner and the saint.
> The Saint moreover turns to God
> God rewards an afterlife wanting naught.
> Knot of a hangman's noose is not akin
> A kin to saintly nature or reward.
>
> Reward for the hangman is in his craft.
> Crafting the rope to stop stretch or break.
> A break of the neck is turned in thirteen."

Reichmann smiles that same sad smile. "A chain poem. You don't hear those very often. So is that how you feel Earnest? Do you feel like there is no reward in heaven for you? That you are neither sinner or saint but merely the hands of death?"

"Good night, Mr. Reichmann."

"Good night, Earnest."

The door shuts behind Earnest. The question echoes in his mind. *Why am I so meticulous with my craft?*

The morning of Mr. Reichmann's death is warm, sunny, with a cool breeze. The summer wind is fresh. The gallows where Reichmann will be hanged is inside the "Barn." The guards and the death row inmates have named it the "Barn" because it is literally a pole barn building. It houses the gallows when it's needed.

Earnest Lauder readies the noose. He runs his fingers down the coil. *Thirteen turns to break a sinner's neck* rings in his head.

"You all set?" Frank Trot steps into the dimly lit pole barn. He is a portly guard with a broad stance and strong demeanor.

Frank's appearance is enough to snap Earnest back to reality. "Yeah." He tugs on the rope. "It's good."

Frank points with his right index finger. "If I were you, I'd make the son of a bitch strangle to death."

Earnest walks down the podium's steps. "I ain't you Frankie."

"I know Ernie. But did you hear what he did to those girls?"

"I did." Earnest wipes his hands on his pants and glares from the corner of his eye. "Straight from his mouth."

Frank's face turns red. "So you know he raped and killed them girls and he don't give a damn."

"Yes sir I do."

"Them girls," Frank's legs begin to fidget. "They were the same ages as Victoria and April. What if Ernie? What if?" Terror clearly grips Frank's body. The before-mentioned girls are his daughters, who call Earnest "Uncle Ernie."

Cool sincerity takes hold of Earnest's visage. He places his hand on Frank's shoulder. "Frankie, if I filled my head with 'what ifs' I'd go mad. Thank God it wasn't Vicky or April and pray to Him to be with the parents of those girls that were murdered."

"Don't it make you angry?" The confusion in Frank's voice matches his face.

"Yes sir." He looks back at the hanging noose. The eye loops under perfectly formed coils. The words *weights on Justice's scales to speak* travel as an escaping thought. "Anger don't solve anything in this situation. It's a waste of energy and time. He's getting what the law says is his due justice. Leave it be at that."

As Earnest passes behind Frank, he swears he hears Frank say, "I hope the bastard chokes to death." The fresh air washes over him and he pushes it out of his mind. His stomach is upset. Tension always grips his muscles before a hanging. It's a role he loves to hate and hates to love.

Ringing of chains forces his eyes open. The warm friendly smile of Professor Reichmann greets him. An urge to return the smile is smoldered by Earnest's thoughts of the noose behind him. This man is a murderer. He need not be greeted with a smile.

Reichmann's voice cracks, "You sleep well last night?"

The first response to fight to escape Earnest's lips is 'Yes sir' but like the smile, he grapples with it. He digs his toes in the dirt and looks down at the aged worn leather of his boots. The black is no longer shiny. It's aged and dusty. The way Earnest feels some days. "No, no Sir. You?"

"Not a wink." The smile flattens. "I figure it will be okay. I'm about to spend a lot of time resting." Earnest isn't sure if that was intended to be a joke. "I thought about you quite a bit."

"Really?"

"Yes." Reichmann nods. "I thought how peculiar it is that you, of all people, have the sort of job you do."

This is the most complex death row inmate Earnest has ever met. "What are you meaning? A hangman?"

"Yes." Chains clang as Reichmann raises his hands to adjust his glasses. "I've come to believe I can see a person's character in their eyes. Even as a boy, I'd stare in the mirror and know mine were the eyes of a killer. With yours…" He squints to get a better look. "Are the eyes of a truly compassionate man. The sort of eyes you see in mother Teresa or Gandhi."

Earnest laughs. "I hardly believe I can be compared to either of them. It's a dramatic comparison, don't you think?"

"Oh, I don't think so." Reichmann is serious. "I think they fit the archetype. When it comes down to the human spirit, it's not as muddy as we'd all like to believe. Sure sometimes there is a gray area but in my book gray only transforms a two sided black and white subject into a three sided one. No Earnest. I don't believe you are a man cut out for this job."

"Really?" Earnest recalls all previous twelve hangings in one blink of an eye. All of them were breaks. All of them used a thirteen turn noose. "I've been doing this a while now."

"You misunderstand." A pause allows Reichmann to regroup. "Why would someone, with as much compassion as you, ever work a job such as this?"

Earnest's lips part to reply with an answer he is miles from knowing. The thought had crossed his mind before. There had to be others out there who weren't bothered by this line of work. Why couldn't someone like Frank do this job? The simple answer, "I don't know." A tornado of ambivalence turns in his gut as he continues, "I guess I don't trust anyone but myself."

The answer seems to please Reichmann. Happiness flushes his cheeks. Frank steps out of the barn and steals it away as quickly as it colored. "It's time."

"To recap," Earnest swallows hard. "We are going to walk you atop the podium. There I'm going to position you, give you a chance to say your last words, then put a bag over your head. It'll be dark as night under there. I'm going to put the noose around your neck with the coils resting behind your left ear." He points to his own ear to demonstrate. "Then you are to take a step forward."

Reichmann nods. "I understand."

The march into the building is a sick ceremony. No matter how Earnest tries to perform the needed action, it always feels like a funeral, wedding or communion. There is something about it that feels too much like a ritual. It shames him.

No matter how they enter and ascend the stairs, one thing is the same, Earnest never looks the crowd in the eyes. He only looks at them with his peripheral vision. If he had his way no one would be allowed to watch.

In the time he and Reichmann were talking outside, a crowd had assembled. Four weeping mothers are tightly held by angry fathers. Reichmann's philosophy about people's eyes draws Earnest out of his shell. For the first time in thirteen hangings, he looks the family in the eyes, each one.

The fathers wear both mourning and anger. They look like they could as easily kill as cry. The mothers' grief is one that could tear the earth's tectonic plates apart. The reporter has a delightful glee in his eye. It's much like a jester. The priest is indifferent, distant and lost in thought.

Earnest continues to scan the crowd as he climbs the podium. Every eye swings like a hypnotist's watch. Instinctive thought places Reichmann into position. Earnest's eyes swing and lock with Reichmann.

In the twisting of color of the cornea and the red veins in the sclera, he can see the killer. It's hidden behind happy eyebrows and a warm friendly smile. It's a cold stare from an ancient evil. It's an evil that, for a moment, Earnest fears dwells in all of our eyes.

Eagerness to finish the task grips Earnest. "If you have any last words, please speak them now."

Reichmann scans the crowd. "I do." His stentorian voice echoes against the tin walls. "I had a speech prepared but looking at this crowd I can't help but be overwhelmed with the need to tell you that it was all far too easy."

A hush falls on the assembled people. It's clearly what Reichmann wanted. "You mockingly cry for children you failed to cling to and protect from harm and I'm the one to be hanged? No, I do not apologize for what I did or your negligence as parents. I know seeing my body hang from this rope and noose will give you little satisfaction or closure because every day of your lives, you will be haunted by what you could have done to protect them from harm."

Anger, mourning, confusion and hatred wash over the crowd. The statement knocks Earnest back a step. He tries to outrun the tidal wave of emotion as he puts the hood over Reichmann's head. The noose is placed perfectly behind his left ear.

With his hands tight around the coils of the noose, Earnest is plagued with the thought of Reichmann strangling to death. Strangling the same way he strangled his last victim. As if Reichmann heard what he was thinking, he says, "Thirteen turns to break a sinner's neck."

Earnest's mouth drops, he steps back, and his palms fall to his thighs. The crowd hushes.

From the stairs, Frank utters, "God, choke the bastard. I want to see him dangle and kick."

The wind is knocked out of Earnest. He focuses on Frank's face, on his eyes. "What?"

"I want to see him suffer." Frank's eyes blaze with a fire reminiscent of Reichmann's. "I want to know he had plenty of time to think about what he did. I want him to think about them girls and how he robbed them of their life. I want him to pay."

The urging in Frank's face matches the crowd. Earnest pictures them all wanting the same grotesque death. He whispers, "Pay more than his life?"

No response from Frank. The fires in the red of Frank's sclera burn hot.

Then it strikes Earnest. The old poem reads, *Reward for the hangman is in his craft.* A perfect answer for Reichmann's final question takes life and breathes inside Earnest's mind. He steps next to Reichmann.

In a quiet voice, that only he and Reichmann can hear, Earnest replies, "The reason why I do this job is thirteen. Thirteen turns to break the sinner's neck. It has to be done perfectly. You can't feel a thing. It has to be painless, what the law says is humane. It has to because…"

83

Earnest pauses and swallows. His mouth is dry. "It has to because I feel remorse for every one, all thirteen."

The black hood shudders as Reichmann exhales.

The words tremble from Earnest's tongue, "Step forward."

Reichmann's left foot plants into the center of the trap door followed by his right. A few gears and weights click in response. Three, two, one and the door drops. The heels lead. Reichmann's shoulders shrug and his hands lift. The body falls. It's the victim of gravity. The noose tightens and twists the neck. There is a snap and Reichmann is dead.

· 13 ·

A scholar, a saint, a revolutionary: **Aaron Behr** is none of these. He is a writer who has written a few novels and even more short stories. This Ohio born and raised writer loves to write. It's a curse. He traded promising careers in a dozen different professions so as to birth his muse and share her to the world. Aaron believes that a life lived is filled with the stories we create and the ones we share. He strives in earnest to do both.

ON THE WINGS OF HELL

BY JAMES S. MCCREADY

Thunder crashed in the darkness above the *Hollander* as a wave dashed over her bow, adding a harsh salty spray to the stinging downpour. The gale force winds shrieked through shroud and stay while the storm-reefed sails, gray against the tar black sky, strained at the yards. Even as sturdy a ship as the Dutch fluyt could be, hull and mast alike groaned beneath the fury of the sea.

Still half-blind from the lightning's wrathful flash, I clung white-knuckled to the main bitts and struggled to belay a loosened line as the keening winds buffeted me about. Heeling with the ship, I turned to see Captain Van der Dekken himself standing stock-still on the quarter-deck, unaffected by wind and wave.

"Mr. Vorhees," he shouted to the First-Mate. "Clew down the heads'ls. This damnable storm pulls us off course no matter what we do."

"Clew down the heads'ls, aye," returned the Mate. "Don't seem like Heaven wants us to reach the Indies."

Another wave crashed over the bow. I turned my face away as seawater drenched me.

"Heaven be damned," bellowed he. "I'll sail on the wings of Hell till Kingdom come if I must, but round the Cape I will. God himself cannot deny my passage!"

I crossed myself, aghast at the blasphemies that spewed from the

Captain's mouth. Several others, wide-eyed and ashen-faced, made the sign of the cross as well. Thunder crashed above us. It resonated through my chest and made my ears ring.

"God forgive him," I shouted to Merrick who hauled away on the line beside me, "and protect us from the storm's fury."

"Heaven hear ye, Jan DeGraaf," agreed the Englishman, "and bless us poor souls that sails with 'im."

"Waterspout," someone shouted, pointing. Lighting wreathed the funnel-shaped spout as it moved across our bow and into the distance.

"Twelve years before the mast," said Merrick, "and never have I seen such a sight."

We looked at each other, and then went back to work, all the while reciting the Lord's Prayer together.

Moments later lightning shattered the top foremast, snapping lines and stays. The mast crashed to the deck atop two hands as the ship heeled, sweeping a third man toward the sea. Screaming in terror, he struck the rail hard and flipped over it.

I belayed the line and ran forward to help secure the remains of the mast. We could not lose it, nor could we allow more men to die this night.

"Help me!" came a panicked cry from the rail. I raced to the rail and found a man clinging to it, fighting to throw a leg over and heave himself aboard. Davy, the cabin boy.

"Hold on, boy," I called out, leaning over to grab his arms. "Bear a hand, mate," I shouted to whoever could hear, "help me get him on deck."

Another wave crashed into the ship, jarring me from my precarious hold and tearing the boy screaming from my grasp.

"Davy," I shouted. Strong hands grabbed my oilskin and hauled me back to safety. "Davy!"

"Too late," said the Spaniard. "He is gone. Come, we must secure the mast."

86

The Bosun raced from the steering deck and took the stairs two at a time. "Captain," he shouted. "The starboard ten-pounder has broken loose. We need more hands to—"

"Take Lars and Olin," Van der Dekken interrupted. "Tell the Portugee to lash the staff and bear a hand—helm can wait. Heave that gun to!"

"Aye, Captain."

Ill news, this. Cannon have been known to smash through to the sea and take the ship with it. I crossed myself again and muttered prayers.

The storm abated sometime after midnight, and most of us went shivering below to shed our oilskins and draw a ration of grog, and then climb bone-weary into our hammocks.

The Mate roused us at eight bells, and after a cold breakfast sent us on deck to consign our dead to the sea and clear the storm's damage.

The Captain stood on deck amidships reading the last rites over our fallen mates. Bright brass buttons fastened his burgundy-colored coat, and the polished silver buckles on his shoes gleamed white. A brace of gold-chased pistols rode in a wide black leather belt. His white-feathered hat sat as square on his head as the yards above him, and his eyes gleamed fierce from beneath thick black brows. Not a whisker dared breach his stern, clean-shaven face.

We grieved for our shipmates, the first to fall this voyage. We also grieved for ourselves, for it could just as easily have been any one of us. This had been poor Davy Weir's last voyage as cabin boy, bless his departed soul. He'd spoken of opening a mill with the money awaiting him in Antwerp. Now it would go to his bereaved family.

I looked out toward the horizon as the Captain continued. The sea danced and sparkled in the golden sunlight, belying the storm that had killed my friends. The ever-present gulls added their cries, which seemed almost mournful to me.

Finally finished, and without even an 'Amen,' Van der Dekken closed the book and nodded to the attending seamen, who tipped the planks forward to commend the shrouded bodies of our shipmates to the deep. Three distinct splashes ended the service, with only fading ripples to mark their final resting place.

After being dismissed, we worked hard until just after ten bells when a cry came from the crow's nest. "Sail, ho," Svensen's booming voice echoed over the ship. "Sail, ho."

"Where away?" shouted the Captain.

"Off the weather bow, east-nor'east."

"Bearing what flag?"

"English, Captain."

Opening his spyglass, he raised it to his eye as the carpenter fastened a new spar into place atop the foremast. He watched for a while, then lowered the glass and snapped it shut. He glanced up at the naked spar.

"Mr. Vorhees," he called to the mate. "Get the riggers aloft. I want to be under sail as soon as possible." He paused. "And man the guns."

* * *

By noon, we had repaired the yards and strung new stays. The approaching ship had now sailed into hailing distance and hauled in her sheets to heave to. I stood near the mainmast, mounting the tackle back onto the yards.

"Ahoy, there," shouted the newcomer in English-accented Dutch. "We're the *Albatross*, out of Portsmouth and homeward bound. What ship and where?"

"The *Vliegende Hollander*, out of Antwerp and Batavia bound," the Captain returned. "Be ye friendly, then?"

"Friendly," came the English captain's reply. "There's little profit in ruining good trade with fighting. Let us leave that chore to our respective navies."

The saints be praised, I said to myself. Let the war stay in Europe.

"Agreed," the Captain stated. "How be the sea ahead for us?"

"Unusual fair, for this time of year," replied the Englishman. "You'll find premium prices in Java."

"Our thanks, *Albatross.*" He pointed to work being done on the foremast. "Be warned sir, all the storms be on this side of the Cape."

"Aye, that we saw last even. Most happy we were to be blessed by St. Elmo's fire at the ending of the storm. They don't call it Good Hope for nothing. Well, fair winds and Godspeed to ye, *Hollander.*" With that, the *Albatross* cast off and hoisted sail, resuming her homeward course.

"Godspeed be damned," muttered the Captain. "And the same to St. Elmo. Let him keep his bloody fire."

Many crewmen traded alarmed glances as the captain turned from the rail. More blasphemy. The patron saint of sailors often blessed a ship with bright blue flame at the tips of the masts and the ends of yards as a good omen. Surely Heaven must now be taking notice.

"Mr. Vorhees, full sail as soon as we may and damn the man that shirks. Three days from the Cape are we, and round it I will before Sunday next or Devil take my soul."

Mr. Vorhees set six of us on the capstan to haul the repaired tops'l yard into place, relieving the men who'd hoisted the new spar. Freshly tarred wooldings, set to keep the mast timbers from splitting, glistened black in the sun. We hauled away not to the tune of a brisk sea chantey, but to fearful murmuring of seamen with hearts heavy as anchors. St. Elmo had not seen fit to bless us with his fire at the end of the storm, as he had the *Albatross.* I feared Captain Van der Dekken's blasphemies had marked us all for a curse.

Soon after, thunderheads formed in the distance, and the Mate swore. "Look alive, you maggots! If we don't outrun that storm, I'll flay the hide from your worthless carcasses."

We flew into the ratlines, climbing aloft to unfurl every square inch of canvas. The *Hollander* leaped forward, running with the wind. Our efforts mattered little for the storm, incredible in its swiftness, soon overtook us.

The sky darkened and the gale force winds sang an eerie tune in the rigging. Strange, the winds carried no scent of rain.

Clouds, darker than the leaden sky they swirled against, spun downward to envelope the *Hollander* within what seemed to be the eye of a hurricane. Dark masses of clouds swirled above, with nary a glimmer of sunlight to bless the slate-gray waters that swatted at our hull. Lightning laced the walls of our prison, sending the distant rumble of thunder across the waves.

Then the thick, gray fog rolled in like a pestilence that crept toward us over the face of an unfriendly sea. The wind died suddenly, and the sails hung limp from their yards. All hands stopped and looked about. Seasoned sailors we were, but none of us had ever seen such an unnatural sight as this. I glanced up at the Captain. He too stared at the creeping fog.

Only the slap of wave on hull and the creak of rigging broke the silence. The calls of seabirds were unnaturally absent—even the gulls had fled. The smell of hot tar hung heavy in the still air.

"Ship off the larboard quarter," called the watch from the crow's nest, and we all turned to look. Full-filled sails had she despite the calm, her masts, yards and spars aglow with what I first took to be St. Elmo's fire, but a hellish red instead of a comforting blue. Merrick and I, along with several shipmates made again the sign of the cross, muttering prayers under our breath. I trembled and wished mightily for a few fingers of rum.

The new arrival hove to alongside and tied up, lending the odor of brimstone to the salt sea air. Its crew set a wide plank to bridge the gap, then its Master and his Mate boarded us without so much as a by-your-leave from the Old Man.

"Avast, there," the captain thundered from the railing. "Who the

Devil d'ye think ye are, barging aboard uninvited?"

"Ye know well who I am and what my business be, Hendrick Van der Dekken, for ye summoned me yourself not long ago."

I stared fearful and dumfounded at the sinister dark-haired man, and crossed myself again. His eyes glowed red like coals of fire out of a sun-bronzed face set with a mustache and goatee. His rich red velvet coat, with its gold buttons and trim, stood out against trousers as black as the darkest night. Gold trimmed his hat, which bore feathers from some bird I'd never seen before. Tall black boots reached above his knees, set with silver buckles of an unearthly sheen.

"I took notice when ye mocked God to his face, Captain. I salute your bold sentiments." He doffed his hat and gave a mocking bow.

"Shall we retire to your cabin? We have business to discuss." The sinister man fixed his unearthly eyes upon me and pointed.

"Since you've gone and lost your cabin boy, Mr. De Graff here will serve us drinks." He tossed his hat to me. "Brandy, man, and be quick."

My heart pounded in my chest as if the man had touched me with the very finger of doom. Fearing to cross myself in his presence, I recited an *Our Father* and a *Hail, Mary* under my breath as I hurried to comply.

* * *

Quaking with fear, I poured brandy into two glasses and placed both them and the crystal decanter on the Old Man's silver tray, then carried it to the Captain's sideboard. I set it down beside the strange hat and handed each a drink, then stepped back a pace. Our unwelcome guest downed his with one swallow, then held his glass up for a refill. As I complied, he grabbed my arm and pulled me forward. I nearly dropped the decanter.

"Are you wondering why you're here, young man?"

Too frightened to speak, I nodded vigorously. He laughed and released me, and then reached into his coat pocket to withdraw a mahogany dice cup set with gold filigree and pearl insets. A triple row of diamonds decorated the lip, with rubies, sapphires and emeralds separating huge pearls banding its equator. He opened a velvet pouch, pouring an ivory dice set with tiny black pearls for pips into his hand. He placed all on the Captain's polished cherry tabletop and sat back. Down went the brandy, and he fixed that ungodly gaze upon me.

"You are a witness," said he. "An *honest* witness that can stand before heaven and declare the proceedings of this day to be true and factual before both God and man." He smiled at Van der Dekken.

"I know you like to gamble," said he, dropping the dice into the cup, "as often as you've tempted Heaven. These are my terms. If I win, you round the Cape and lose your soul. If not, you keep both your soul and your oath."

Three rounds they played then, dicing for the Captain's soul. What game I do not know, for I am not a gambling man. Judging by faces, Van der Dekken won the first round, the Dark Master the second.

The last round, though, I swear I'd never seen a man squirm and sweat as the Captain did that day. I held my breath, fearing what the Captain's fate would mean for me and the crew. The Dark Master shook the cup and poured out the dice, his eyes never leaving the Captain's face. My only clue to the outcome was the briefest closing of his eyes and the slightest sag of his shoulders in relief.

The Dark Master laughed, then downed another glass, which I refilled. "Well played, sir, well played. You have kept your soul, and your life." He put the dicing gear away, tossed back one last brandy. He snapped his fingers and pointed to the hat, which I fetched him quickly and backed away.

"But this curse I pronounce on you," he said, putting it on and setting it to a rakish angle. "Though on the wings of the storm you shall fly, never shall you round Good Hope. The bodies of yourself and your crew shall not die, nor shall your ship rot. Never shall ye see port again, nor put solid earth beneath your feet. As you have sworn, not till Kingdom Come. And of your crew shall there be thirteen dead and thirteen damned with seven saved alive."

With that, the Dark Master and his mate returned to their hellish vessel, which sailed away into the eerie fog. I shivered, chilled to the bone.

"Captain," I said trembling, "you've damned us all to a living hell. By all that's holy, let those who wish it depart in peace, I beg you."

Van der Dekken regarded me in silence for a moment with a look that could have stripped the flesh from a shark. He grabbed my jacket and hauled me close, snatching the simple wooden cross from my neck and hurling it over the railing. He smelled of tobacco, sweat and rum.

"Not a word of this to anyone," he growled, his eyes boring into mine. "Not a word or I'll slice your gizzard stem to stern and use your rotting body as a figurehead!" With that, he shoved me away with such force that I fell to the deck.

A breeze began to blow, filling the sails and dispersing the fog. Lighting crackled in the distance, and roll of thunder resumed as the wind picked up. Captain Van der Dekken stalked outside.

"Mr. Vorhees," he shouted to the Mate, "Get these lazy fishwives back to work. We've yet a thousand leagues to sail before we rest."

Bad luck rode our wake thenceforth. Accidents continued, killing and injuring several shipmates. Two of the hottest-tempered men got into a gambling brawl, and the Spaniard killed the Frenchman with a belaying pin. They tried and hung him the next day.

Next we lost our direction. For seven straight days, we wandered aimlessly in the Cape's waters. The Portugee swore by God he held a steady course, not wavering from the Captain's orders. But every morning, the sun rose in a different place. Sometimes off the larboard quarter, sometimes off the starboard bow. In a fit of rage and curses, the Captain keelhauled the man. By the time they dragged him against the barnacles along the length of the ship's keel, we'd lost most of him to sharks. What we pulled back up at the stern didn't live long.

After that, the Old Man himself took whipstaff in hand, steering a course true to the binnacle through the night. But same as the dead helmsman, we woke to find the sun dead astern the following morn. I looked at the Captain then, and his eyes met mine in a warning glare. I prayed to God for a way off that accursed vessel.

Many a mate bade me tell what happened in the cabin that afternoon, but I could not—*dared* not speak of it. Murmuring began, and soon after talk of mutiny. A few days later, Abram Bruett, the most outspoken of them, drew his belt knife and charged the Mate.

"Bruett, no," I shouted, racing to block his path. Shouldering me aside, he closed with the Mate as I crashed to the deck.

Drawing those gold-chased pistols, the Captain shot Abram dead on the spot with one, then spanned the crewmen on deck with the other. Every man stopped dead in his tracks.

"Mr. Vorhees, summon all hands."

"All hands on deck," he shouted, his voice breaking like the pistol shot over the silent ship. We gathered below the quarter-deck where the Captain stood waiting.

"All hands present, sir," the Mate reported a few minutes later. He stood by the quarter-deck ladder.

Captain Van der Dekken leaned on the larboard swivel gun, which he kept loaded with two pounds of musket shot. "Rumors of mutiny have reached my ears, men. Seaman Bruett attacked Mr. Vorhees not five minutes ago." He pointed at the corpse lying in a pool of blood.

"Look ye; for the same can happen to any man here." He glared at every single one of us, holding my gaze the longest. I turned away, glancing back toward the boat. When I caught his eyes again, they narrowed into a look mixed of hatred and anger. I prayed he would catch my meaning.

"Such a breach of maritime law I will not endure," he continued, his voice a rasping growl. "My final word on the matter is this. At Seaman DeGraaf's request, any man that refuses to sail with me will be put into the jolly boat and set adrift with naught but the clothes on his back and a fortnight's food and water. That coward shall forfeit his pay for the voyage, and his gear shall be auctioned off at port. Those brave souls remaining loyal shall receive triple shares. Now," he said straightening, "let any man wishing to forego our company gather at the boat."

We looked at each other for a few moments. Merrick and I traded glances. 'Twas the answer to our prayers, we knew, so we walked astern and stood by the boat. Over the next several minutes, by ones and twos others joined us, until we numbered seven. The others stared sullenly at us as we readied the boat and lowered it. Some cursed and insulted us. Mr. Vorhees and the quartermaster themselves brought the supplies from the hold and dumped them at our feet. The Captain watched, reloading the spent pistol and replacing it in his belt. He crossed his arms and waited, his face darkened by contempt.

"His hands are too near them pistols for my taste," Merrick whispered to me as we loaded the boat.

"Let it be," I returned. "He cannot stop us now."

"What if 'e wants the jolly boat back?"

"He'll not need it again, I think," I replied, heart filled with sadness and pity for the accursed men.

Several minutes later, we climbed down into the boat and made ready to shove off. I sat at the tiller, and while the others extended oars, Captain Van der Dekken leaned over the rail and hailed us.

"Our visitor's words were lies, DeGraaf," he called, mocking. "I only have twelve men, and with them I can still make the East Indies and back."

The Dark Master's words echoed in my mind as the starboard oarsmen pushed off from the *Hollander*. "Thirteen dead and thirteen damned with seven saved alive."

I stood and looked the Captain squarely in the eyes. "Yourself, sir, makes thirteen."

His shocked countenance paled, eyes wide. Then he straightened at the rail and scowled.

As we pulled away, the dark clouds swirled above us and the breeze picked up. We hoisted sail and ran with the wind, indescribable relief washing over me. With lifting heart I looked back one last time at our former vessel. The same eerie red glow that had lit the Dark Master's ship now engulfed the ship that Merrick called the "*Flying Dutchman*."

• 13 •

James S. McCready is a native of Columbus, and grew up an avid reader. At some point he decided to try his hand at writing, but quickly found out that a pen works better. He is a long-time fan of classic tales, adventure stories and science fiction. He also enjoys history, but at present has seen only the last fifty years.

THE CAT LADY
BY DEBORAH CHEEVER COTTLE

Cora Mann called out to her cats. "Here, Kitty, Kitty, Kitty." She was pleased to hear that her voice carried no trace of the anxious dread that coiled and squeezed at her heart as she led her feline flock out onto the cold back porch.

Large flakes of snow floated in the air, and already a patchwork of white had settled on the frozen blades of grass. Cora opened the door and several cats charged out like gleeful children, chasing wildly after snowflakes as if they were tiny butterflies. Others walked carefully, lifting each foot with high, dainty steps. Cora laughed as she watched them, unwilling to stifle the joy she always felt with the winter's first snowfall.

Cora left the door cracked open as she waited for the cats to finish outside. She loved the crisp, clean bite of the frigid air on her face and the symphony of sounds that rose to greet her. . .the rustle of dry leaves, the call of a cardinal, the purrs of the cats as they reentered the house.

For that brief instant it was a day like any other and Cora welcomed it gladly. A sense of peace and happiness flowed through her, a childish delight in the wonders of the world. But reality soon cut through the rich tapestry of joy in which Cora had wrapped her life. A team from the Department of Animal Control would soon be there.

She closed the door and climbed the porch stairs with unusual slowness, her hands flying like thin, fragile birds to clutch the heavy folds of her sweater. Cats hovered around Cora's feet, rubbing gently against her and against each other in a comforting ritual.

Cora bent slowly, ignoring the sudden burst of pain that shot through her spine, and scooped up a huge black cat that had been nudging away smaller cats in a bid for Cora's attention.

"Buddy, you're a big old bully, you are," Cora whispered tenderly as she cradled the animal against her chest, rocking him the way she had rocked her only child so many years ago. "I'll miss you, Old Fella," Cora said as she lowered Buddy back to the floor, then brushed away the tears that slipped over the wrinkled valleys of her face.

A bell, hanging from the curtain rod on the kitchen door, tinkled brightly as Cora turned the large enameled doorknob. The cinnamon scent of freshly baked cookies filled the room. Although she wasn't hungry, Cora knew she should eat. She washed her hands and ladled out a bowl of soup from the pot that simmered on the stove.

She had just finished her lunch when she heard the soft rumble of a car making its way up the long country drive. Cora's attention flew to the window. She didn't recognize the car, but she knew who the driver would be.

Ellen had come home.

Cora knew she had every right to be angry with her daughter. Ellen had been the one to set the wheels in motion—wheels that Cora knew would disrupt the very essence of her life.

"How dare she. How *dare* she." Cora had uttered those words for days after the animal control people had made their first visit, days when anger and desperate hurt had battered her body like a storm. But even then she had known. Ellen truly thought she was doing the right thing when she had called Animal Control. She wanted what was best for Cora and for that Cora was grateful.

She hurried towards the door, wanting to spare Ellen the awkward decision of whether to knock or come straight in as she had done countless times when the old farmhouse was her home, too.

Ellen stood tall and straight beside her airport rental car, her eyes flashing questions that needed but one answer. Slowly, widely, Cora spread her arms. She could feel Ellen's relief as she walked and then ran towards her. Ellen's hair, already starting to gray, brushed soft as velvet against her cheek as Ellen bent to her embrace.

"You don't hate me?"

"Of course not. You're my daughter," and she held this woman, still a girl to her, even closer.

"Mom, let's get you inside. It's too cold for you out here."

A sudden and surprising sense of peace settled around Cora. Ellen was home and the nameless fears that skittered about the edges of her heart would be held at bay. She would take advantage of their time together, no matter how limited it might be.

Cora led the way into the house, nudging away the cats that crowded around the door. "Have a seat and I'll get us some tea," she said as Ellen draped her coat over a kitchen chair.

Cora busied herself with the kettle and cups. As she worked, she was reminded of other cold winter days when she had stirred a pan of hot chocolate on the stove while Ellen played in the snowdrifts outside. Ellen would come in red-cheeked and runny-nosed and they would sit together at this very kitchen table, drinking hot chocolate and laughing and talking of wonderful things.

Now Ellen was grown and Cora was an old lady fixing tea rather than hot chocolate, but she knew there were still important conversations to be had.

Cora brought the tea and a plate of sugar cookies to the table and slowly settled herself into a chair. "Is Jamie at home?" she asked. Like her mother, Ellen had been blessed with a child late in life.

"He's going home with a friend tonight after school."

Cora nodded, her finger tracing smoothly around the delicate gold rim of her porcelain teacup as she thought about the direction she wanted the conversation to go.

Deciding there was no time to beat around the bush, she took a deep breath and said, "You know, when you and Jamie visited last month, and I let the cats stay in the house—I did it for Jamie. I thought he'd like them. He was your age. That's what I was thinking."

"My age? What do you mean, Mom?"

"He's seven. You were seven, too..."

"When we first got Kitty," Ellen finished, as a soft gleam of understanding flooded her mind.

"Jamie hardly knows me, Ellen. He was so young when I'd seen him before. I wanted him to have fun this time. I wanted him to make some memories of me."

When Cora had learned that Ellen and her son, Jamie, would be flying out for a short visit last month, she had decided instantly that the cats would stay. On other visits she had sent them off to the barn, sure in her knowledge that Ellen's now ex-husband wouldn't have appreciated her pets.

But last month's trip was for Jamie. Cora knew he would love the cats. It would be like living in a pet store and such an experience would print enough memories to last a young boy a lifetime.

The morning of that visit she had brushed each cat till it gleamed and had even tied little ribbons around the necks of those who would stand for such nonsense. And she had been right. Jamie's face had glowed with enchantment when he saw the cats.

Ellen watched Cora silently. Her mother stared straight ahead, her eyes teary and distant. She seemed to be lost in a faraway place and Ellen wasn't sure if she was drifting on a sea of memories or scanning the horizon of her future. She felt a desperate need to bring her back, to have her mother with her before it was too late.

"Mom," she prodded gently, brushing back a thin strand of hair that had drifted across Cora's cheek. She was tempted to snap her fingers or flag her hand up and down in front of Cora's face. Instead she called again, a little louder this time, "Mom."

100

Cora blinked and turned her eyes slowly towards her daughter. "I'm sorry." A tiny smile rested tentatively upon her lips. "I was just remembering about Jamie and the cats."

Ellen smiled too as she let her memory drift with her mother's. "He did love the cats, you know."

Cora rose and walked to the window. "Then why, Ellen?"

Ellen shuffled her thoughts rapidly, searching for the perfect culprit on which to lay the blame.

"Mom, look at me."

Cora shook her head and Ellen heard a sniffle as her mother's hand rose to cover the tears on her cheek. Ellen moved to stand behind her mother, her hands resting on the sharp blades of Cora's shoulders.

"Mom, *thirteen* cats. It's just too much."

Cora turned to face her as she spoke. "So what is the right number, Ellen? One? Seven? How many cats should a person have?" The words flew like cold, sharp pieces of flint and Ellen felt the pierce of each one.

"You know there's not a right number. But thirteen is wrong. It's not a healthy situation."

"Is my house dirty, Ellen? Do these animals look sickly?"

A mixture of guilt and regret began to kindle at the base of Ellen's stomach. Although she knew her mother's question was rhetorical, she had to admit to herself that despite the cats, the old farmhouse was as clean and fresh smelling as always.

"It hurt me when you took Jamie and went to stay at that hotel. I had your rooms all ready, you know."

"I know." Ellen spoke slowly, placing the words like eggshells on cotton. "We did still have our visit though."

"Visits and meals at a hotel just aren't the same. You know that. I'd wanted us all to be together here at home."

Cora stopped quickly, clamping her lips in a tight line. She was over the boundary. She had made her point and there was no need to play the martyr. From the look in Ellen's eyes she knew her daughter was already hauling enough guilt to fill a boxcar.

"I'm sorry, Mom. I'm really, really sorry. I overreacted. It's just that I worry about you. It's a lot of work to take care of thirteen animals and you're out here in the country, all alone."

"I'm not alone, Ellen. I have the cats."

Ellen shook her head slowly as the irony of the statement struck home. She started to chew absently at her thumbnail and Cora, in a gesture made automatic by her years of motherhood, reached up to take Ellen's hand and hold it in her own.

"I wish like anything I'd never called those animal control people, but..."

There was no need for her to finish the sentence. They both knew the ending.

The wheels of bureaucracy had been put into motion and there was no way to put on the brakes.

Cora took a deep breath as she gathered her strength and turned towards her bedroom. "I suppose it's time to get myself ready. After all, I'm going to be a TV star, you know."

Ellen put her hand on her mother's arm, momentarily halting her movement and the falsely chipper tone of her voice. "Maybe it's not too late to call off the TV part, Mom."

"Oh, no. I want them. I called them myself. I want this to go out on the air and I want as many people as possible to see it."

Cora's eyes shown with conviction. "Whenever they have a story like this the station gets swamped with calls from people wanting to adopt the animals. It's the only decent chance of making sure all of these guys get good homes."

"You know what people will think, don't you?"

Cora smiled and for the first time a tiny twinkle appeared in her eyes. "That I'm a crazy old lady. The Cat Lady—that's what they'll call me." Cora chuckled. "I *am* a Cat Lady. And I'm 80 years old. Most people assume I've got a few screws loose on that basis alone."

Ellen knew there was no arguing with her mother. Once she had made up her mind there was no turning back. She smiled and gave her mother a quick hug as she stood beside her. "Then let's get ready."

Ellen washed the teacups and saucers while Cora ran a warm cloth over her face, wiping away the unfamiliar tightness the dried tears had left on her skin. A Channel 6 News van was coming up the driveway as Cora slipped a bobby pin into a stray wisp of hair.

Cora joined Ellen at the window and they watched as a huge man in brown coveralls opened the van's sliding door and began to unload equipment. A trim blond bundled in a calf-length wool coat stepped down from the passenger's side.

Cora felt a jolt of excitement. "That's Peg Muncy!" She grabbed Ellen's arm, kneading it unconsciously as she talked. "I watch her every night on the news."

Ellen smiled down at Cora, her excitement like a burst of sunshine after a spring rain.

They met Peg at the door and Cora was pleased to note that she was even prettier in person.

"Hello, Mrs. Mann. I'm Peg Muncy from Channel 6 News."

Cora shook the offered hand with as much firmness as her arthritis allowed. "It's nice to meet you, Miss Muncy. This is my daughter, Ellen. Please come in." As Ellen shook the reporter's hand, she marveled at the way her mother's natural sense of graciousness had taken all traces of awe from her voice.

"We thought we'd set up inside and get some background shots of the house and cats first, if that's OK." Peg's gaze traveled the room, making rapid notes.

Cora nodded and hurried to pick up a young calico that was about to take a swipe at Peg's nylon covered ankle.

Peg's rich laugh filled the room. "Don't worry," she assured Cora. "My own cats have already snagged them up."

"You have cats?" Cora felt the warm comfort of hope settle around her body.

"Two of them." Peg reached over to rub her finger behind the calico's ear before adding, "They're two of my best friends."

Cora cast an optimistic glance in her daughter's direction. Ellen's gaze locked into hers, returning a look of encouragement.

Cora and Ellen watched from the sidelines as lights and equipment were put in place. Cords snaked like a freeway system through the house. The cats pounced and batted at them, never realizing that this was but the start of a new adventure.

Suddenly, as if on cue, all noise and confusion stopped. A man— this one wearing jeans with one knee torn and the other faded to a pre-hole gray—moved behind the camera. Peg traveled slowly through the room, talking into a microphone as the camera followed her progress. Cora felt a sense of pride and relief as she heard words like "immaculate" and "healthy" being used to describe her house and animals. And then just as suddenly as the confusion had stopped, it started again.

"The animal guys are here," the huge man announced as he grabbed equipment and disappeared outside.

The animal guys are here. The words slid like an icicle into Cora's heart. The excitement the TV people had brought evaporated like tendrils of mist. The heavy, sick feeling returned to her stomach.

"They're just going to get a few outside shots of the control truck's arrival."

Peg's words sounded slow and very far away, as if coming to Cora through an echo chamber. Black spots swam across Cora's eyes and the room began to sway around her. She stumbled slightly and reached out for Ellen's arm.

"Mom!"

Cora let herself be led to a chair. She took a sip from the glass someone had put into her hand. The water trickled out the corner of her mouth and painted a black streak across the front of her blue blouse. Slowly the spots receded and the room stopped spinning. Cora reached into the deep pocket of her skirt and retrieved a crumpled tissue.

"What a crazy old fool I am. Can't even drink without spilling." The words had the spunky tone of self-deprecation meant to negate the message and as Cora began to sponge at the damp spot, Ellen breathed a sigh of relief.

The animal control people were entering the house now, unescorted and uninvited. They were on a government mission—one that had become a public interest story no less—and that, Cora supposed, gave them the right to abandon social mores.

They brought with them a small flotilla of blue plastic crates. A young man, hardly more than a boy, and a girl with stringy hair and a scattering of colorful tattoos began putting cats into these mini-prisons.

The caged animals yowled fearsomely as they were stacked like crates of potatoes by the door. It was only the fact that the two workers seemed to be handling the cats with gentleness and care as they captured them that allowed Cora to bear the emotional turmoil that belted her body in black waves of pain.

A heavy woman who had been watching the proceedings from the sidelines now crossed the linoleum, her ridiculous high heels clicking with the sound of authority. She bent to peer briefly into each cage, revealing a wide fringe of gray-white slip beneath the red polyester of her dress.

"Twelve," she proclaimed as she stood up and ran a hand down the bulges that circled her middle like a topographical map. "Seems like we're missing one."

Cora knew Buddy, her big, black cat, had not been caged. She wondered for one giddy moment if two unlucky superstitions might cancel each other out—if being number thirteen might bring good luck to a black cat. The thought had no sooner crossed her mind than the young girl entered the room with a yowling Buddy clutched in her arms and hope gushed from Cora's body like a mortal wound.

Cora stretched out a hand to cradle Buddy's massive head. He calmed instantly, the yowl replaced by a gentle purr as he rubbed against the comforting knots of Cora's knuckles.

"Mom, if you'd like to keep one of the cats I'm sure it would be O.K."

Cora's heart thudded rapidly at the possibility. She had almost started to lift Buddy from the girl's arms when some innate instinct took over and she heard herself saying, "No, it's best if they all go together."

The girl stuffed Buddy into a cage and then headed to the door with him. Cora followed behind.

"It's cold out there, Mom. You'll need a coat," Ellen said as she realized that Cora intended to stay with the cats as they were loaded into the truck.

Cora stood limply, letting Ellen slip a coat over her arms and fumble with the large oval buttons that were becoming more and more difficult for her hands to work.

The outside air burned as they breathed, but the snow had stopped. Cora and Ellen stood at the outskirts of the action, watching the events that would forever change their lives.

And then it was over. The animal control truck was pulling away and the news crew followed. "Let's go back inside, Mom," Ellen said, her hands already guiding Cora as she walked across the slippery ground and back into the house.

A suffocating silence wrapped around them and Cora fought desperately to put away the feeling of loss that gnawed at her soul. "Will you be staying overnight, Ellen?" she asked.

"I wish I could, but I have to get back to the airport for an eight o'clock flight." She wrapped her mother in her arms and felt the stroke of Cora's hand against her hair in a gesture so gentle it made Ellen's heart ache.

"Are you O.K., Mom?" she asked as she gradually released the hug.

"I've had a good life."

106

Ellen's gaze caught the clock as she straightened, and by the time the question left her lips her thoughts were already on drive times and check-in hassles. It wasn't until later that night, flying somewhere over the vicinity of Des Moines, that the inappropriateness of Cora's answer had registered in her mind and cold worms of panic had slithered into her stomach and begun a slow dance.

For now she only nodded and announced that she really needed to be going. They walked to the door and hugged once more.

"I love you, Mom." The words came easily.

"I love you, too."

Cora watched as twin tunnels of light pushed into the thickening darkness, bobbing when Ellen's car hit ruts as it turned and headed back down the long drive. She rested her head briefly against the cold window and then turned to face her house.

The emptiness crashed into her like a weight. She could feel it hovering around her as she made her way back to the kitchen. She washed the cups and decided to forgo supper.

In a move that surprised her even more, she decided to skip the six o'clock news and her own few minutes of stardom. She wandered restlessly through the house, her arms hugged protectively around her chest as if trying to defend herself against unknown, evil forces.

She flipped on the TV in time to catch *Wheel of Fortune*. She tried desperately to focus her attention on the screen, but her hands fluttered restlessly in her lap, hungering for the touch of sleek fur. Cora decided she didn't much care if there was a vowel in the puzzle tonight. She turned off the TV and prepared herself for bed.

She lingered at the window a minute before giving up the day. The clouds had cleared and hundreds of stars were scattered across the rich blackness of the night. She felt a burst of joy at the night's beauty as she let the curtain fall loose, then slipped into bed.

Her hand reached over to set the alarm clock, but from the same instinctual well that had told her to send Buddy to a new home came the

107

knowledge that she would not be needing a wake-up call in the morning. She pulled back her hand and rested it upon her chest.

A comforting sense of peace tucked around her. Cora sighed and closed her eyes.

· 13 ·

Deborah Cheever Cottle has had stories published in two previous CCC anthologies, *While You were Out* and *Columbus: Past, Present, and Future*. She has also recently completed a suspense novel for which she is currently seeking representation. Deborah lives in Westerville, Ohio with her husband. They enjoy visiting their son in Seattle. Deborah can be reached at debbie.cottle@gmail.com.

A BAKER'S DOZEN

BY JENNY L. MAXEY

I love my job—the aromas of sweets baking in the oven, the feel of raw dough squishing between my fingers. And, best of all, I get to mix business with pleasure.

* * *

The radio came on, stirring me from my sleep. The alarm clock flashed 3:00 am. I rolled to my side. The bed was empty, only an indentation left behind. I rolled to my back and stared up at the ceiling. "Jessie's Girl" by Rick Springfield was playing. The song reminded me of the summer when I was ten. My mind flashed back to a specific moment—I was playing in my yard. The rain from the night before had left a thick layer of mud in its wake. Being a baker even then, I squatted to the ground and filled old pie tins with mud. The little girl from next door came over and squatted by my side. She always liked to be my assistant. Wisps of blonde hair blew across her face in the wind. Her blue eyes connected with mine as she asked, "So, what are we baking today?" Bettina and I made mud pies until the mud dried to dust. The sun began to set and I knew she needed to get home. Before I could mention it, her dad was walking quickly in our direction, pumping his arms. Bettina started to cower behind me. Her father, silent, grabbed a fistful of her hair and pulled her across the yard and into the house. It was several days before I saw Bettina again. Where was that little girl today? I looked back at the clock—3:15 am. It was time to go to work.

It was still dark out when I arrived at the bakery. The lights were already lit within, the bell hanging from the doorknob tinkled as I stepped inside. Flakey croissants and cheese danishes with juicy cherries oozing from the centers filled the glass case, awaiting our early bird patrons. This means that I've missed my wife Nicolette. She's always up early, so I rarely get to see her busying herself in the kitchen. Rolling the dough just so and forming the crescent shapes on the baking sheets. The way she raises her finger to her lips after touching a hot croissant from the oven, and says, "Oh my! Zis iz zo hot!" in her French accent.

In the adjacent case were rows of glistening, glazed doughnuts. Plump rings lightly dusted with fine sugar and others with thick, pink frosting and rainbow-colored sprinkles. A growl emerged from my stomach. The sweet circles were evidence that my wife Brianna had also completed her work for the day. It had been weeks since I'd seen Brianna, so I was sorry to have missed her. I snatched a glazed doughnut from the case and headed back to the kitchen.

The deep fryer's scalding oil hissed and crackled. Brianna had forgotten to turn it off before she left. As I reached to shut off the fryer a faint humming from the back corner of the kitchen drifted across the room. I flipped the switch to the fryer and followed the tune to where my wife Annabelle stood, swaying her hips to her little melody. A bin of flour sat open, cracked egg shells were scattered on the counter, and a strainer of freshly rinsed blueberries dripped water onto the floor. I reached my arm around Annabelle and dipped my finger into the sugary muffin batter she was holding close to her chest.

"Come on, that's just unsanitary," she said.

"A little taste won't hurt anyone," I replied and swiftly stuck my batter-covered finger into my mouth.

She scrunched up her face into a pout and then she raised her eyebrows, bidding a review.

110

"It's perfect, honey. Maybe add just a pinch of salt."

"I'll give you a pinch of salt!" She thwacked my arm with the back of the spatula.

"Now *that's* unsanitary," I said.

Annabelle flung the dirty spatula into the washbasin. She leaned into me, sliding her hand under my arm in search of a clean spatula. She held her body close, pecked me on the cheek, gave me a smirk, and went back to her mixing and humming. Oh, that Annabelle, so quick and flirty. She's constantly keeping me on my toes.

I decided to start working on a birthday cake order that was going out in two days. I turned away from Annabelle as she poured the batter into a muffin tin. I collected the dry ingredients, measured them out, and gently sifted them together, making sure all the lumps were removed. Sifting is such calming work. I got lost in the moment, watching the flour and the sugar slowly combine and then stream into the mixing bowl like sand in an hourglass. I whisked together the wet ingredients and combined them with the dry, stirring until the two became one.

My hands continued to work as my mind went elsewhere. The memory from this morning was forcing others to push their way forward. We were both thirteen, taking a Home Economics course. I was setting up our station when Bettina strolled in. "So, what are we baking today?" she asked.

"Bundt cake," I replied.

She pushed up her sleeves and gathered her blonde hair into a high ponytail with a blue scrunchy. Once we completed the batter, I stuck my thumb in the bowl and licked it clean. Just as quickly, she stuck her own finger in and popped it into her mouth. "Mmmm that's good!" she said as her eyes grew large, a smile stretched across her face. We reached for the utensil drawer. The backs of our hands barely brushed. She recoiled and pulled her arms in tightly, tucking her hands under her armpits. I looked at her face and couldn't read it. Disgust, surprise, anger, shame—a wave of emotions quickly swept away. She emptily gazed downward and didn't speak the rest of class. I wasn't sure what I did, but I always regretted that I couldn't fix it.

My thoughts were interrupted by the smell of smoke stinging my nostrils. I ran to one of the ovens where a thick cloud of smoke crept around the edge of the door. I grabbed a pair of mitts and pulled out the blackened rocks resting in their metal pods. The muffins were ruined. Annabelle was gone.

The front door jingled. Before I could go to the storefront and tell the customer we weren't open yet, my wife Helen stormed into the kitchen.

"I could smell the burning from outside! That's a good way to draw in customers—with the savory smell of ash!" Helen said.

"Oh, don't worry about me. I'm fine and the place didn't burn down. Was that you who came through the front door?"

"Yes, it was me. And I'm going to assume it was you who left the door unlocked yet again."

"I guess I must've. Sorry dear. Won't happen again."

"Good. I just stopped in to make sure the supply order went out today."

Helen strode into the side office in the storefront and slammed the door. Dear, dear Helen. That woman gets under my skin, but she's a keeper. She's the only one who knows how to manage the books and keep the business in line. I guess I could also hire an accountant for that, but, then again, an accountant won't offer the same perks that Helen does.

I went back to the cake order and spooned out the silky batter into greased pans. As the cake rose like two golden suns on the horizon, I began to crave cornbread. It wasn't just any cornbread. This particular cornbread was sweet and warm. When torn apart, it sprouted long, orange, cheesy tendrils. Once the bread settled onto the tongue, jalapeños released shocks of spice and heated the breath. Although I've tried to make this cornbread several times, the cheese never stretched as far and the jalapeños never shocked enough. Only one person could make this cornbread: my wife Maizey. It's been years since Maizey has shown herself. She departs just as quickly as she arrives, but during her brief visits, she is as memorable and unique as that cornbread.

"Hello, handsome," came a seductive whisper, followed by a squeeze in my bum that jolted me from my visions of Maizey. The mystery woman covered my eyes with one hand and softly spoke into my ear, "Try something for me." She slid her finger between my lips. The rich taste of chocolate consumed my mouth. The thick batter coated my tongue. A hint of caramel swirled through the batter. The sensuous taste bursting from this brownie batter could mean only one thing: my wife Desiree.

I spun around and yanked her close. She hopped onto me, wrapping her long legs around my waist, and ran her fingers through my hair. She pressed her forehead against mine, as if she were trying to read my mind. The bulge in my pants would surely make it easier.

"So whatcha think of my brownie mix?"

"Mmmm hmmmm," was all I could muster.

Her two front teeth tenderly bit the corner of her bottom lip. "I'm sure they will be better once I heat them up," she purred. "Do you like my brownies hot?" The timer on the oven dinged.

"Damn." I begrudgingly placed Desiree down on the counter. "Hold that thought."

I pulled the cake pans from the oven, flipped them from the pans onto a cooling rack. When I turned around, Desiree was gone and a mixing bowl of brownie batter rested in her place. I rushed out of the kitchen to the storefront. The office door was open. I peered inside. It was also empty. Helen must've left with Desiree. Why were these women slipping out of my hands like butter?

I looked behind the counter of the storefront and my wife Ida was counting the tender in the cashier's drawer. Was it that time already? I looked out at the picture window and the soft yellow light of morning was beginning to pour through.

"Good morning Ida."

"Morning." She kept her head down, focused on counting coins.

Ida didn't have any baking skills, but she was magnificent with our customers and at keeping the kitchen clean and organized.

"I'm going to grab a few of Grace's pies from the back and set them out for display."

Ida looked up slowly from her handful of change and stared at me.

"I'm sorry. I'm so sorry. It just slipped."

"I told you never to mention her name around me again."

"I know. I'm so sorry."

"I think it's time you get rid of her. I think she's been stealing from the register again. Besides, she never cleans up after herself. Yesterday she left her dirty pie pans in the sink and spilt vegetable oil, which made a greasy mess all over the floor. Do you know how hard that is to clean up?"

"I'll have a talk with her the next time she comes in."

Ida scowled and went back to counting the change. She's never liked my wife Grace. I think, more than anything, that Ida is jealous of Grace, but this stealing thing was something I would definitely have to investigate.

I went back to the fridge in the kitchen to remove two of the pies that Grace made yesterday, one apple and one coconut cream. Both are her specialties. Next to the pies were my wife Lucy's cupcakes. Lucy is the youngest and is still harnessing her talent. The frosting on the cupcakes was sloppy and running down the sides. It looked like a child had finger-painted on them. I sighed. I decided to put some of the cupcakes on display instead of the pies, at least until Ida calmed down. I would hate for a coconut cream pie to go flying into the face of an innocent customer.

I scraped off the frosting, replacing it with a new coat and headed back to the storefront. Ida glanced at me from the corner of her eye and smiled when she didn't see pies in my hands. I smiled back. I neatly arranged the cupcakes in glass domes on the top of the pastry cases. Customers began to trickle in, which was my cue to go back and bake some more.

With my cake order still cooling, I decided to work on various breads. My wife Gabriella was in the bakery yesterday. She spent the afternoon preparing several kinds of dough and placed them in the fridge to rise. Today was a great day to make bread. It hadn't been rainy lately, which would add moisture to the air and weigh the bread down. It also wasn't too hot, where the fats in the dough could melt and make the dough too sticky to knead.

I whiled away the rest of the morning and through to the late afternoon with Gabrielle's dough. Braiding the challahs and marbling wheat with rye. I rolled the dough flat, folded it, and pressed my fingers along the center to form baguettes. I plumped the dough and squeezed it into loaf pans. I twisted dough into pretzels and slashed diagonal lines into other dough to make it bloom in the oven. The kitchen was filled with the fragrance of bread.

While some of the loaves continued to bake, I went to check on Ida. She was going through our wedding cake design book with a customer.

"Hey, Ida? I'm going to walk around the block and pick up some coffee. Do you want anything?"

She looked up from the design book. "I'm okay. Thanks though." She turned back to the customer.

I walked out of the storefront and turned down the sidewalk towards the coffee shop. I always take a few minutes for myself after making bread. I need time to stretch my neck and legs and warm my fingers from the chilly dough.

As I started my walk back with the coffee, my thoughts returned to Bettina. We were eighteen. Even though we both had a license, on nice days we enjoyed walking home together after classes. She was

115

clutching her calculus textbook under her arm and was excitedly chattering about her plans for after high school. "I can't wait to move away from here. I'm going to France and becoming a pastry chef. I'll make wonderful things with lots of butter. My treats will be so rich, that even *you* won't be able to eat all of it!" She poked at my belly and giggled. I didn't have a large stomach by any means, but I was getting a little soft from tasting my own creations.

When we reached our block, there were police cars and an ambulance in front of Bettina's house. She dropped her book and ran closer to where a crowd was beginning to form. The police had cuffed her father and were walking him to the cop car. His eyes fell on Bettina, and he glared as if she had been the one to summon the police. He spat in her direction. The EMTs wheeled a stretcher away from the house. A sheet was draped over it. Bettina wailed like an injured dog. I threw down my backpack and wrapped my arms around her from behind. She continued to scream and tears spilled down her face. She wildly kicked her legs, trying to free herself from my stronghold.

Bettina distanced herself from me after that day. A few weeks later we graduated high school, and Bettina flew to France according to plan. Where was Bettina now?

By the time I got back from the coffee shop, Ida had put the "CLOSED" sign up and locked the door. How long had I been gone? Fifteen, twenty minutes tops. It was curious. She rarely leaves, especially if I'm not there. I unlocked the door and the bells tinkled behind me as the door swung closed. Ida wasn't in the front or in the office. I went back to the kitchen. My bread was out of the oven, cooling. A new aroma floated throughout the kitchen, the smell of chocolate chip cookies.

I looked around the corner toward the back of the kitchen. Her back was to me. All I could see was her blonde hair rippling around her shoulders. But I knew; chocolate chip cookies were the signature of my wife Jillian. I walked up behind her and wrapped my arms around her tiny waist. I nestled my chin on her shoulder and touched my lips to her neck.

"Jillian, my sweet," I cooed into her ear.

Faster than a stroke of a whisk, she whirled around and smacked me across the face.

"It's Kate! Why is it that you can never—I mean never—tell us apart?" Jillian's twin said.

"But, it's chocolate chip cookies!" I was reaching and she knew it.

"Wrong. Those are sugar cookies. I always make the sugar cookies. See!" She pulled the baking sheet out of the oven and tossed it onto the counter. The cookies shuffled around, some of them falling to the floor. Sure enough, those were sugar cookies. Damn. I was losing my touch. My wife Kate stormed out of the kitchen and into the storefront. I decided to give her a minute to cool off before I followed.

After a moment, I walked to the storefront to find her. As I looked around, I heard sobbing. Behind the pastry cases, slumped on the floor, my wife sat weeping; her shoulders bobbed up and down. I ran toward her and knelt down by her side. I held her arms and tried to meet her eyes.

"It's happened again, hasn't it?" She looked up. A smudge of flour spanned her cheek.

"Yes, Bettina."

"Have they all been here?" She looked around at the different baked goods and already knew the answer.

Bettina nodded to affirm her answer and then looked at me. Behind the tears, her blue eyes shimmered. In those eyes, I saw all thirteen of my wives – Nicolette, Brianna, Annabelle, Helen, Maizey, Desiree, Ida, Grace, Lucy, Gabrielle, Jillian, Kate, and, my one true love, Bettina. I pulled her into me and cradled her across my lap like a child. Her head rested on my chest and her tears dampened my shirt as I stroked her hair. We stayed just like that—in a small heap behind the pastry case—until the orange sunset streaming through the picture window faded to darkness.

I had followed Bettina to France. I gave her space, but only enough to let her come back to me in her own time. Growing up, she mostly kept to herself, and her parents obviously paid little attention to her, so the personalities were hard to detect at first. But, as they became stronger, more defined, and began calling themselves by different names, I knew it was more than mood swings. Her doctor said that dissociative identity disorder typically begins with a traumatic event in childhood usually involving sexual abuse. Sure, it isn't easy being married to someone with the disorder, but we make it work. I know each woman intimately. The way they laugh. Their funny takes on life. The way they tie their apron strings. The way they kiss. I am amazed by how far the heart can stretch. How it can love thirteen different women equally and yet so differently. I've learned to love each woman as she appeared. But, I also remember the little girl stooped beside me, helping me make mud pies. No one knows her like I do. No one can love her like I have always loved her.

• 13 •

Jenny L. Maxey is a published author in multiple anthologies including CCC's *While You Were Out: Short Stories of Resurrection* and *Columbus: Past, Present and Future*. Her story "A Baker's Dozen" is dedicated to her brother Jody Struble because he said it was his turn (and it rightfully is). Jenny also would like to give a special thanks to Laura Shilliam. Jenny lives in Central Ohio with her amazing husband Douglas and dog Sophie. You can find out more about Jenny's ongoing projects and publications by following her on Twitter @JLMaxey.

FARAH'S GIFT

BY KRISSIE LYNCH

The girl clung upside down to a spare tire underneath a lumbering truck that lurched into a bombed-out pothole. She grimaced when her backside raked the edge as the truck crunched up and out over hunks of metal shards. Her peripheral vision registered an AK-47 assault rifle trigger nestled on the road, orphaned without a handle or muzzle. Her arms burned and her legs shook as she struggled to hang on.

She dared not cough for fear of detection. Instead she slowly worked up enough spit to drool out the road grit that threatened to reach her throat. She silently convulsed as the charred contents of the pothole splashed back into her mouth and reminded her of what had passed.

The Iraqi girl tells me this, and I silently record her words. I am a bilingual counselor, working for a relief agency based in New York and it is my job to work with young refugees displaced by the war in Iraq. Even though the U.S. has now pulled out, the children still arrive. What I hear mostly are the sweet details of everyday life that are still part of a child's world—memories that the children desperately cling to and use to fill up conscious memory so that the violent and tragic experiences of their recent past do not surface. They tell me of their friends or a special treat they received for their last birthday. Rarely do they tell me what really happened.

* * *

On the drive home, I cannot stop hearing the clear voice of thirteen-year-old Akilah. I still see her delicate brown hands tucking gleaming black hair back into her head scarf as she told me her story. She had been wearing jeans and a long-sleeved Aeropostale t-shirt—from the shelter, no doubt—but her head had been completely covered, which had made her eyes all the more expressive.

At home, after getting dinner started, I try to classify her situation in terms my profession uses; I try to assign a diagnosis, a treatment plan and prognosis. Really, all the children I see have the same diagnosis of Post Traumatic Stress Disorder, but the treatment plan must vary depending on the trauma, so as not to create more of it by talking about too much too soon.

My daughter Jenny enters the room, sliding on the hardwood floor on stocking feet. She sees my computer and tries to sneak a peek.

"Uh uh, not allowed," I say, minimizing the screen.

"But who did you see today?" she asks, peeling off the socks, which are black on the bottom.

"A beautiful girl, like you," I say.

She balks, disappointed, because sometimes I tell her a little bit more about the children.

I grab the compost container and hand it to her. "Go empty this, and give the heap a turn."

Jenny is also thirteen; she sighs heavily as she dramatically swoops the container into her arms and heads directly outside, without stopping in the garage for the compost fork. She runs past the squash and beans and dumps the contents of the pot onto the steaming compost heap. On the way back, I see her stop and pick some of the slightly unripe orange cherry tomatoes. She holds one up to the afternoon sun and tries to see through its translucent skin. She is quite proud of these tomatoes that she started in her science class earlier in the spring and that now, in the mid-July Ohio heat, look like a fireworks display. Her tan cheeks balloon as she crams a handful into her mouth and pierces their softness. I chuckle as the warm juice squirts out the sides of her lips. She is like me: she likes the not-too-ripe taste: light, acidic and just sweet enough. She reaches for more and I know her hands, from picking, will smell like the taste. In front of me, the notes I took during the intake interview with the Iraqi girl seem other-worldly.

* * *

Akilah remembered the smell of her village from the taste of the pothole. Her sister Farah had cried, "Dare you to run home!" It was a privilege for them to be going to school outside their home and they had been told to return each day as quietly and dignified as possible. Akilah told me that she was a little jealous of her sister, younger by two years and unconcerned with her carefree image. But this day was the last day of school so she had laughed and charged after Farah, hiking her burka up to her knees in order to reach full stride.

She smelled it even before she careened around the corner to their street, crashing into her sister. Farah stood straight and stiff, eyes uncomprehending and arms leaden against the now still folds of her burka. Akilah pushed past her.

The familiar smell of stew and wood and baking brick was masked almost totally by a stench that made her gasp and her eyes water. She held a hand over her mouth and nose and frantically searched for her mother and father. There were the caved-in walls of their home, frosted with glass, purple smoke billowing out of the shattered panes. She thought she glimpsed her mother's clothing beneath the rubble but she could not be sure and the heat prevented her from moving closer. She became aware of shouting men, many with cloth masks over their faces, their angry eyes an inadequate cover for their own horror. To run now would not have been undignified but the girl realized that Farah could not move. Akilah refused to leave Farah and continued to hold her tightly even as she felt them both being hoisted onto a cart by one of the men. They were held down by a combination of sweaty, dirty arms and the handles of semi-automatic weapons.

"Did you know who those men were?" I had asked Akilah, when she paused. "Why they would want to hurt your village?"

The girl looked past me, at my framed diploma on the wall, indicating that she had heard me only by saying that asking herself those questions was the only thing that had kept her terror at bay. They were easier to think about than the images she had seen.

Over the next few days she realized they had been taken to the city of Bagdad, a place she had, in her childhood exuberance, begged her father to take the family. It was a much bigger city than any near her village, and her father had always promised a trip if the girls did well in school.

The circumstances of her first visit were inconceivable compared to what she had imagined. They were told they were taken to an orphanage but it soon was apparent that the "chaperones" were not kindly people. In order to avoid being beaten, she and Farah did as they were told and tended to a small group of younger children. Farah concocted games just as she always had, but did not participate. Akilah worried that this was not because her sister had decided to be dignified at last. They never spoke of their flaming home or parents until one particularly gunshot-riddled night. They lay on makeshift pallets with the other girls and Farah said, "I will not be a good wife; even the smell of a cooking fire now makes me sick." Akilah silently agreed but wondered if Farah was worrying about the wrong thing. She had noticed that some of the older girls had been taken away. She tried to lighten Farah's apprehensions, "If your husband dared you, you'd waste no time!" It pained Akilah to see that Farah's face registered no reaction to the teasing.

In private Akilah did not joke. Her mind reeled with competing worries. Out of this chaos of intermittent attacks and gunfire, she discerned that it perhaps was the nonrandom threats that should be feared the most. Was she orphaned and homeless, with the sole responsibility now for a younger sister? Would she be taken like the other girls? (Did it matter that her periods had just started? If so, how could she trick them by pretending they hadn't?) Were she and her sister of the wrong religion? What was the right religion? She overheard the harsh voices of some of the guards one night, "There is too much attention now that they are here." The girl ached to understand. Were there rules for war? How could she possibly keep herself and her sister safe if others had so many reasons to harm them? Her thoughts sputtered along with the artillery and she finally concluded that there were new rules and ancient rules and yet there were no rules.

* * *

It is hard for me to believe I heard this entire story only this morning. I stick my head out the back door and remind Jenny she has a guitar lesson at four. It pains me to think of her suffering like the Iraqi girl. Her life is filled with softball, tree houses and teen TV shows that favor shameless overacting and a light grip on reality. It is perhaps not good for me to bring my work home, for me to mix these worlds. I tell Jenny to mind her sister—I know Jen hasn't even noticed her in the sandbox. Jenny's flexible, muscular frame is now bent into a downward-facing dog yoga pose and she merely squints at me, with upside down eyes and flopping ponytail, and then twists to watch her younger sister arrange her sand-sticky Barbies around the edges of a brownie-pan pool. I type in the girl's case number on an assessment template and continue reviewing my scribbled notes.

* * *

Akilah told me she watched her sister fold inward to avoid what she could not withstand, like certain flowers in the light of day. After a while Farah simply stayed curled in bed, leaving Akilah to mind the children all by herself. Because she dreaded staying in the noisy city center with the children, she convinced their captors—as she now secretly named them—that the children would settle down and sleep better if they could play outside. They were permitted to go on an outing to a safe park nearby. The captors walked behind Akilah and the group of children, pretending to be soldiers patrolling the neighborhood, but Akilah knew if she took one step off the route, she would hear a barked order and perhaps feel again the pressure of a gun to her back.

The park was in a neighborhood that was one of the oldest near Bagdad; its residents had lived peacefully together through this war and others. As she nipped and tucked at the children to keep them moving, the girl wondered why some areas were so untouched by hate and destruction and others so completely ruined.

The children pressed around her and pleaded for a game. She attempted to do what Farah could do so easily. "Pretend you're on a safari," she finally suggested.

"What are we hunting?" they said, their eyes brightening. Her sister would have come up with some clever idea. In exasperation, she said, "Why don't you hunt for things that will make Miss Farah feel well again?"

The children lined up to show her what they found. "This rock is a gun, see?" one grimy boy proclaimed proudly. Akilah caught her breath when a delicate girl held out a few pithy fig branches and whispered, "Miss Farah can put these on her cooking fire to make it smell good."

Akilah awoke the next morning from an uneasy sleep suffused with memories of home. She lay very still to hold onto the vanishing sensation of that happy, predictable life. She turned to give Farah the fig branch she had forgotten in her pocket, but Farah's pallet was empty. The girl searched their living area, then ran out in the street. All she could think of was why had they taken Farah and not her? Far ahead up the street she spotted Farah, but then saw her bolt into the buzzing market street and disappear under the thundering wheels of an armored vehicle.

Akilah had stared down at her folded hands as she told me, shamefully, that at first she felt nothing but anger that Farah had dishonored their family. Then, after the anger, she felt nothing. She was emotionless and groundless. She could not eat because her stomach lurched at the slightest thought of her sister. She described how she touched her sister's pallet in the powder-hot daylight and still powerfully felt her sister's presence. Felt the lightness and joy of a sister that could not find a balance between the life she had known and a life she could not now pretend she didn't know. Akilah unfolded her hands as she spoke as if to grasp again for that essence. The girl lifted her eyes to rest gently on my face and said, with a voice as silvery and delicate as a child's charm bracelet, "She could not stay in that world."

* * *

I eye Jenny, now rolling over to pluck some pale baby green beans. She takes only the tender sweet ones that are not much bigger than a toothpick. I wonder if I purposely expose her to some of the stories of my brave young clients. I feel a familiar surge of insecurity as I remember how I used to marvel at the girls who paid their way through college by waitressing. Their confident grace as they maneuvered their way through the minefield of rudeness, urgencies, compliments and come-ons. People said they must be so organized to get all their studying done and still have time to work. They wondered when they had fun. They felt sorry for them, but I was jealous. I wanted to know what they knew, to have that set of skills, that confidence.

I again bring my gaze back inside, fill in a few of the fields on the assessment form, and wonder how I can sum up the Iraqi girl's serendipitous and courageous story into any category except its own?

* * *

Akilah chose another market day and woke early enough to be sent with only one captor, who yawned and grumbled and stopped as soon as he could at a tea stand. Akilah had continued walking, slowly at first, pretending to carefully pick the most unblemished fruit, and then had slipped into the crowd. This day it was not fruit that the girl picked but a departing caravan of trucks.

The truck she chose bumped on past the smoky crater. The gritty saliva seeped through the girl's lips and she tasted her village, her mother and father. She tasted her sister, whose escape used a similar route but ended too quickly, too completely. Akilah was not crushed under wheels but tucked near ones carrying barrels headed for the Gulf.

* * *

I snap the laptop shut, stare for a moment at my simmering dinner. Then I open the sliding screen door and call out, more forcefully than I mean to, "Jenny, go get the pitchfork and turn the compost right now, and then come in and get ready for guitar."

· 13 ·

Krissie Lynch lives in Northeastern Ohio, though snaking through her veins and stories are residues of time spent in Pennsylvania, New York, Michigan, Massachusetts, London and her beloved Montana. "Farah's Gift" began during a commute from a business meeting in Columbus, Ohio to an impromptu writing retreat in upstate New York. It is her first published story.

THE THIRTEEN PERCENT GRADIENT

BY JULES KNOWLTON

It has been determined that slippage occurs at a gradient of thirteen percent or greater. Therefore it is mandated that any and all construction on said gradient or higher requires permit application and review. Road surfaces at an angle of inclination at or above the thirteenth percentile must be constructed as per the directive set down by the Pennsylvania State Board of Engineers to control drainage and possible erosion.

As he peers through the windshield at the darkening road ahead, a sign depicting a tiny yellow vehicle comes into view. The image hovers above squiggly tire marks and the words "Slippery When Wet." The sign, glimmering through the rain, reflects briefly in the headlights of the car, then is gone. *Yeah, I'll bet it's slippery, cause it sure is wet,* he thinks as the car cuts a swath through the water. He had been going about fifty but now the car is laboring up the slope of the mountain and he cuts back on the speed. They won't make it to the cabin until well past midnight. To top it off, it is pouring. *Damn, a weekend in the rain. God, this had better be worth all of the trouble. It might not be so bad if the sex holds out, but if we get tired of each other, then what?* He turns the wipers up another notch and has to strain his eyes to see through the gloom. He follows the reflective lines demarking each side of the road and sees the bend up ahead. Looking back at the sleeping form of Charlotte on the bench seat, her relaxed figure setting up a cozy tableaux in his mind, he fights the urge to pull off to the side. The most beautiful girl at Penn State is asleep in his car. *Maybe they could have sex in the car? No, no!* He wants it to be special. That's why he planned this trip, taking advantage of the break in the semester, a chance to see the fall leaves, snuggle by the fire.

It hadn't started well. Charlotte had a cold and she complained of a sore throat, her weight shifting from side to side as she waffled on about going. Her packed bag slung over her shoulder belayed her protestations however, allowing Justin to attribute them to cold feet. He too had felt nervous about going. "You can sleep in the car on the way there. I have an extra blanket," Justin had said, taking her bag. Maybe she was a virgin? He hadn't thought of that, unconsciously feeling his pocket for the extra condoms. He hadn't brought any special lubricants or creams. What if things really didn't work out? They would be stuck at the cabin together for the rest of the weekend. Perhaps he should rethink his timing. Hold off on the sex until Saturday night, that way if things turned awkward, only the drive home on Sunday would be uncomfortable. God, there were so many variables. Maybe, they just shouldn't go at all? They could have sex in the dorm instead. No, that wasn't the way he wanted it to play out. It had been an investment of three months, three months that he had wined and dined her, getting ever closer to the elusive goal. Sex in the dorm? No, not good enough for this girl. The cabin it would have to be.

He snatches one last look at her prostrate form and makes the turn, down shifting then applying the gas, smoothly transitioning up the steep hair-pinned road. The tires catch, sending up spray. The rain is coming down harder and he cranks the wipers as fast as they can go. Peering through the windshield, his palms are sweaty on the steering wheel. He glimpses the next turn coming up too fast and brakes. The car skids as he cranks the wheel. *Damn, that was close!* Charlotte stirs and mumbles, "Are we getting close yet, Justin?"

"No Babe. We've got about another half hour to go."

She manages a tired "Um," and falls asleep again. He doesn't even glance back; all of his energies are focused on the road ahead. *Damn, I just can't see.* He brushes his hand across the glass in an attempt to clear away the condensation. The tires of the car roll over debris. Beneath the wet surface, the road has become uneven. Water is running down the embankment on his left. It ripples across the road, pulling dirt and small stones with it. The tires jolt again. Now the car is shaking as he drives over the rough terrain. Afraid they are no longer on the road, he strains to see the edge and slows the car to a crawl. Something slams into the side. Startled he punches the brakes. What could they have hit? The tires spin for a moment as the car pitches and stops. There is a sudden clatter of rocks against the side door. Justin grips the handle and yanks at it. The door won't budge. *Could they have veered into the side of the mountain?* Through the sound of the rain he can hear the spattering of mud, as more debris seems to be piling up against the left side of the car. Alarmed now, he tries to force the door, leaning on it with his shoulder, it still won't open. There is a loud crashing sound coming from overhead and he feels the rear end of the car tip and slide sideways. He kicks at the door in panic.

"Justin?" Charlotte asks, sitting up in the back seat. His hands are white-knuckled on the wheel as he turns it in an attempt to right the car, which is now beginning to slide towards the edge of the road. The metal screeches and crumples as the car tilts, slides, then rolls onto its side as if a giant hand is lifting from underneath. The car hangs for a brief second, its right side still bound to the level surface of the pavement. In an attempt to make sense of the situation, he dangles sideways, one hand still manipulating the steering wheel while the other keeps pulling at the handle of the door. Then the car begins to topple off the edge. With a jerk it flips upside down leaving him suspended by his seat belt; the roof moans and crumples slightly. In spite of the belt, his head slams into the ceiling. Slowly, then gathering speed, the car starts to slide down the mountain. His knuckles tighten and he shuts his eyes.

"Justin?" Charlotte cries in alarm. "Justin!" She screams. "Justin!"

Her voice, like a dim radio signal, registers in his brain as if from far away. He can hear a note of angry accusation in its urgency and panic. It throws him into suspension as its underlying tone registers the familiar incrimination, "You fucked up again Justin!" *It's true, your life does pass in front of your eyes,* he thinks, as he recalls his name endlessly repeated in a similar cadence by his parents, countless teachers and coaches. Even his best friend Tyler, for the past fifteen years, has screamed out his name in the exact same way.

"Justin! Justin! Dude, wake up! Class is over man." Justin remembered raising his head, his neck complaining as Tyler gripped his shoulder and shook him awake.

"It's over?"

"Yeah, you slept through almost the whole thing." Tyler looked disgusted. "How are you going to pass this course if you fall asleep every single time?"

"I can't understand a word this guy is saying. Where do they get these Professors from anyway?"

"Osaka, I think. Look, it's calculus, you don't have to understand what the guy says, but you do have to know how to solve the problems he puts up on the board."

"You took notes didn't you? I'll copy yours and look up how to solve them later."

"I don't know man. Hey, don't you have chem lab or something next?"

"Oh shit!" Justin began to gather his books, knocking several papers to the floor. It was then that he looked over and saw her, Charlotte, slowly lifting her backpack to her shoulder. She was getting ready to leave but looked vaguely in their direction, and just like that, after two months of trying to work up the courage to introduce himself, to say something, anything, it happened. The words just popped out of his mouth.

"Hey! Don't you have chem lab too? We better get going or we're going to be late," and shooting a grin at Tyler, Justin picked up his books and joined the girl the both of them had rated the best-looking girl at Penn State. Justin knew he had won before he had even started. He cast one last look in the direction of his friend. Tyler's eyes were wide with envy, his mouth forming the perfect "Oh." Justin let out a laugh as the door to the classroom closed with a bang.

Bang! The hood of the car smashes against a tree, its branches whipping the windows as the car takes a one hundred and eighty degree spin on its top, debris and dirt raining down on the undercarriage. Jolted into consciousness, Justin squints through the pain and lets go of the wheel. He wraps his arms around his head, urine spilling into his pants. A large boulder smashes into the car breaking the right side windows and launching the car again, flipping it. It turns over and over through a sea of noise. The airbags finally deploy, but Justin, his brain thoroughly shaken, sees and hears nothing, not even the rain as it falls on the overturned earth above them. The momentum of the mountain, quivering in a rain dance, ceases five hundred feet below.

There was this time in high school when the linebacker for the opposing team rushed the play, hitting Justin in the chest with his shoulder, forcing him to the ground, knocking his breath out of him. For a moment Justin is lying on that field, trying to breath in the crisp scent of fall vegetation and earth. His chest hurts. As he takes several gasping breaths, his head clears and he realizes he is resting not on turf, but the inflated air bag. Everything is quiet. The car has resumed an upright position and he is sitting firmly in his seat. He wonders how long it has been like this. He does a mental scan of his body starting at his toes, trying to regulate his air intake in an effort to calm himself and stave off shock. Aside from his hurting chest and his wobbly head, Justin feels miraculously intact. He unbuckles his seat belt but finds himself pinned by the bag. Reaching gingerly to his right he unlatches the middle compartment. His fingers search around until he finds a pen; grasping it, with all his might he plunges it into the air bag and, turning his head so as not to breath the noxious contents, he waits for the bag to deflate. It's dark. The wipers are still and he can't see the headlights. The windshield is cracked and impenetrably black, but the glimmering lights of the dash are still on. The windows on the right are broken out and dirt has piled in on the passenger-side seat. Dirt seems to be covering the entire surface of the car. He yells, "Help!" It sounds pitiful. "Help! Help!" Nothing. *Where is Charlotte?*

Charlotte Barnes. Justin took note of her on the very first day of physics class. It was a big class but he paid attention when her name was called. "Charlotte Barnes." She sat in seat E11, on the same row as Tyler and himself, just further over. Justin and Tyler analyzed all of the students in each of their classes; it was sort of a game. In a large class like physics, they tried to figure out which of their classmates were serious like they were, pre-med like they were, bound for success like they were.

"Ok, so who do you think will be at the top of pre-med by the end of the semester?"

"The guy sitting in seat B9."

"For real?"

"Yeah, he's sitting front and center. His laser eyes are glued to the prof like he shits Bible verses. Totally him, besides I happen to know his dad is a surgeon at the University of Pittsburgh Medical Center. How about you? Who do you think will take the honors?"

"The engineer type, D8, with the facial hair and the sweater. He looks to be about thirty. I'll bet he has a pocket protector."

"Dude, that's so cliché."

"Yeah I know, but it's always the geeks with the pocket protectors. Then they make money, ditch the glasses and marry super models."

"Speaking of women, girl with the hottest tits?"

"Seat D2, hands down."

"D2 it is."

"Girl you most want to hit on?"

"C10."

"C10? Really? Your standards are slipping, for me it's G8."

Justin had to strain his neck to look back. "OK I'll give you that one."

"Overall, most beautiful chick in the physics class?"

"E11." Justin didn't even stop to think.

Tyler leaned over and stared down the row. "Sweet Jesus," he said. "That is one hot-looking woman."

"Am I right? She's in my chemistry class too. She's got to be pre-med. Dude, I've got to talk to her."

"No way! She's way out of your league, even my league. I think she must be the most beautiful girl on all of campus, like in the entire University. She's hands-down the most beautiful girl at Penn State."

"Stop staring. And stop salivating."

"A man can only dream," Tyler remarked.

And so Justin had merely sat and observed her for two whole months, every day in physics, every day in chemistry. There was one day she didn't show up for class, and Justin's world slowed to a crawl as he went over in his mind what could have prompted the miss. Was it another guy, another better-looking guy? Had she transferred? By the end of day he had rendered himself despondent over a woman he had never even talked to, despondent over Charlotte.

Charlotte! He remembers. He reaches up and finds the overhead light; it gives off a faint glow. He turns to look at the back of the car. She is lying face down. Her upper body is on the floor. Her hair covered

133

with dirt. Her legs are splayed over the back seat. He knows instinctively something is wrong. "Charlotte?" He calls out. "Charlotte!" He throws a leg between the front seats, the car groans with his movement and he stops. Unwilling to send it down an unseen slope again, he carefully grasps both seats with his hands and slowly maneuvers himself into the back. He casts a shadow over her lifeless form. He can barely see her. "Charlotte?" he whispers. Gently he reaches down, grasping her by the shoulders. Crouching, he lifts her up and turns her around. Her arm flops down by her side and her head drunkenly falls on her shoulder. Justin brushes the wet dirt from her face. "Charlotte?" Her mouth is slightly open as are her eyes. Justin fights the urge to vomit, instead he screams. He shuts his eyes tightly and screams. Letting her body fall back, he pauses only for a moment then moves swiftly to the front of the car. He sits in the seat, staring forward. He sees his reflection in the windshield. *You did this!* Justin yells and punches at the glass until his knuckles are bloody. With tears streaming down his face, he lowers his head onto his shaking arms and sits for a long time.

God damn it! God damn it! Why, why, why? Why is this happening to me? I want to die! No, no I don't. He's having trouble thinking clearly. Justin focuses on controlling his ragged breathing, suddenly remembering the signs of asphyxiation. In all likelihood the car is completely buried. He has to get out of here. He has get help. He reaches in his pocket for the cell. He hits the button. It glows to life. It's working. *Yes!* He dials 911.

"911. What is your emergency?"

"Ah. Hello, there's been an accident. I've been in an accident..."

"Hello, 911 Emergency. What is the nature of your emergency, please?"

"I've been in an accident, a mud slide or something on Route..."

"911. What is your Emergency?"

"Can't you hear me? I've been in an accident, my girlfriend is hurt."

"911. If you are not in an emergency situation, please hang up."

"No! Look! Oh fuck it!" He flings the phone against the dash, gasping, tears running again down his face, now in frustration. *Stop! Stop! You're going to use up all of the air in here,* his brain is telling him. He reaches down for the phone, his fingers shaking. The screen is cracked and blank. He hits the button again; it flickers to life. He breathes a sigh of relief and dials his home phone number. "The call cannot be completed." He dials again and sees the same message on the screen. "The call cannot be completed." *I don't have time for this shit! A text. I'll send a text. To who? Mom and Dad? They'll never read it. Who knows where I am? Tyler. I'll text Tyler.* "In accident! Please send help! Send help! Charlotte might be dead!" *Charlotte is dead. No! No! No!* He hits send. The phone flickers again, then dies. Justin lets out a long sigh. Did Tyler get the message? He rests his head against the deflated airbag. He's getting tired. He has to get out of here. He tries the horn; it lets out a plaintive moaning noise. The airbag has all but nullified it. He has to get out of this car or he will die here, that much is clear, possibly in a matter of hours or even minutes, who knows? He pushes on the door again. The car creaks and sways slightly, the dirt shifting along the glass on the driver's side window, but the door still will not open. Justin feels light-headed. He has an idea, a deranged idea. He knows he can make one last effort before it's over. If he's going to do anything, it has to be now, but if he exerts himself, the end will come faster. *I'm going to die in here anyway, might as well do it sooner than later.* He turns and faces the back of the car, straddling the center console in a crouch position. *Just like football,* he thinks. Pressing against the seats, he braces his arms on the roof and begins to throw his weight from side to side, leaning in with his hips. The car begins to slowly rock, complaining with every shift. If he can release the car enough to send it sliding down the mountain again he might just have a chance. Slowly he is gaining some momentum. He has to keep it up. He strains and feels nauseous and fights to suck the air into his body. Justin feels the car beginning to incrementally break free, the sodden dirt sliding down the window with each movement. He shifts, and the particle current begins again and again. The car is tipping. He looks at Charlotte, lying still where he has dropped her, her body mimicking the motion of the car, rocking back and forth. Her head is turned slightly toward the back seat but tilted upward as if in ecstasy, her eyes open.

Her eyes open, the kiss, long, deep and slow had lived up to his expectations. God, he couldn't actually be falling in love with this girl, could he? They hadn't even had sex yet. But man, was she easy on the eyes. She was nice and shy and very smart and seemingly had no idea of the effect her looks had on the opposite sex. He liked her and suddenly he wanted to protect her. Protect her from guys like Tyler, who might be his friend, but when it came to the opposite sex, he was a jerk.

"You know, she could just be using you Bro, a girl like that, with a guy like you? All I'm saying is get the goods while you can. Cause she finds something better, man, she's gone."

But after three months of dating, being more careful and solicitous than he had ever been with any other girl, she was still with him and this weekend they were going to have sex. He just knew it, and it was going to be great because he loved her and he was pretty sure she loved him.

By the next morning, the rapidly moving storm, with its wind and massive downpours, has dissipated. Emergency and government officials are trying to assess the full extent of the damage. There has been flooding along the banks of several tributaries and roads have been washed out or rendered impassible in seven counties. Power is out in over one hundred thousand homes. Brian McCluskey and Ted Raines of the Pennsylvania Corps of Engineers stand on a ridge across from the newly formed ravine and survey the landscape.

"Will you look at that? The whole side of the west slope is just gone. The slide started from that apex there and kept going all the way down. Amazing!"

"It's wiped out three switchbacks. We'll have to come in with the heavy equipment just to get the road cleared. It could take weeks."

"Why weren't retention measures put into practice here?"

"I suppose because the slope wasn't deemed steep enough on the west face."

"Well, just look at it now. If that's not steep enough to warrant a mandate stipulating control, then I don't know what is?"

"What is that down there?" Ted points.

"Down where?"

"Right over there." He leans in, directing Brian's gaze. "See? Is that a car?"

• 13 •

Jules Knowlton has degrees in Mass Communications and Architecture. She has practiced architecture in several states and has worked in both ceramics and sculpture, all the while writing, developing various personal projects. With the encouragement of the McConnell Arts Center Writers Group she began writing full-time and is currently working on two novels and a collection of short stories.

KEEPING TIME

BY AARON WYCKOFF

When Michael unlocked the door to his shop, he was fifty-seven years, two months, fourteen days, nine hours, and twenty-three minutes old—exactly twenty-four hours older than when he had unlocked it the day before. It constantly vexed him that he could not be more precise, but his birth certificate failed to specify what second he had been born and his memory, while exceptional, was certainly not *that* good.

Michael stepped inside, the bell above the entrance greeting him with a cheerful, high-pitched tinkle, repeating itself as he closed and locked the door again. It was still sixteen minutes and forty-five seconds until the shop opened to the public—time enough to get everything ready.

Immediately upon entering, he was surrounded by his friends, each one ticking softly away, dividing time into discrete moments, measuring eternity. His eyes surveyed the narrow shop, squeezed between a used book store on one side and a ceramics studio on the other in what was now being called the "Historic Downtown" district—not to be confused with the much newer and more active downtown along the state route, three streets over—the shop's depth barely made up for the lack of width. But for Michael, the shop continued to be ideal, small enough that he need not worry about hiring any help, and the rent still inexpensive due to his foresight and a twenty-year lease.

Along the left wall, two sets of shelves, one near the front of the shop and the other near the rear, supported dozens of mantel and table clocks in a myriad of shapes and forms. Between them, twenty or so hanging clocks adorned the wall, while a half-dozen tall cases stood in a stately row along the back wall, governing the room with the regularity of their sweeping pendulums, self-appointed nobility presiding over their lesser brethren.

A narrow counter ran half the length of the room to his right, its glass display revealing a small assortment of more expensive and collectible timepieces, along with a variety of pocket watches and an arrangement of antique clock keys. Behind the counter, a single shelf bore only five clocks, including the centerpiece of his collection and the only clock in the shop not for sale, a French Empire mantel clock dating to 1807. Michael's eyes settled on his pride and joy, and his ears easily picked out its tick, not so much because it was distinctive or unique, but rather because it was running a half second slower than the other clocks. He was not at all surprised. The clock had lost half a second every day since he acquired it, six years, nine months and seventeen days ago. He had spent hours examining it, trying to find that microscopic adjustment that would allow it to keep perfect time, but the problem lay in the manufacture of the gears more than two hundred years earlier. Michael often thought that it chose to run slowly simply to be obstinate, or perhaps to goad him into an action that he would forever thereafter regret, but so far he had managed to resist its insidious lure and had refused to attempt any alteration to its original mechanisms.

"Good morning, Kronos," he said, addressing the charcoal gray cat who sat expectantly in the center of the room. Like silent pendulums, green eyes tracked his every movement, and the nearly inaudible rumble of a purr began in anticipation of breakfast.

Michael carried out his opening routine quickly and efficiently, moving to the back room to hang up his coat, pop the lid off a small tin of cat food and scrape it onto a clean plate, and exchange the full plate for the empty one on the floor.

Kronos eyed the food dubiously, then stared up at Michael.

"Yes, I know you prefer your dry food, but that is for supper, as you are well aware. Breakfast is canned food or nothing, just like every day."

His ritual show of displeasure complete, Kronos bent to the plate and started to consume what the can proudly claimed to be "a delightful combination of seafood favorites."

"Although, perhaps on Friday I can find some special treat for you. Do you realize that we first met four years, eleven months, and twenty-nine days ago? I do not know when your birthday is, as you have never seen fit to inform me as to that fact, so I think we should celebrate our first meeting instead."

Kronos glanced up briefly from his breakfast and gave Michael a slow blink, which he elected to take as assent. It was just as well, considering that he had already purchased a new catnip mouse for Kronos to celebrate the occasion, along with a small bag of crunchy treats.

Michael washed and dried the dirty plate, leaving him fourteen minutes still until opening. He finished his routine, turning on lights, laying out the tools he most commonly needed, transferring cash from the safe to the register, and then at last meticulously adding half a second to the French Empire mantel clock. With exactly two minutes to spare, Michael closed his eyes and reveled in the perfection of the timepieces around him, all ticking away in unison.

As four of the clocks started to sound Westminster Quarters, Michael unlocked the door and flipped his sign to open, soaking up the explosion of sound as every clock in the shop began to chime, bong, or cuckoo the nine o'clock hour.

The morning went slowly, as was quite common, especially on a Wednesday. Two customers picked up finished clocks, another dropped off a gorgeous Nineteenth Century E. Howard and Company black walnut tall case that had suffered the indignity of a coat of dark shellac at some point and needed refinishing, something that would fill his time nicely on Sunday when the shop was closed. One woman entered, a runny-nosed child dragging at her arm, inquiring about digital clocks, only to stomp out in disgust when Michael assured her he would never be caught dead selling such an abomination.

It was still twenty-three minutes until noon when a rather breathless man entered bearing a Bahnhäusle cuckoo clock. Kronos, who had been dozing in a sunbeam in the front window, immediately perked up and came over to investigate, cuckoos being a particular favorite of his.

"I hope you can help me quickly," the young man gasped. "I bought this clock from an antique shop last week, but it won't keep the right time. It's supposed to be a gift for my parents' fortieth wedding anniversary tonight. Is there any way you can get it done today?"

Michael lifted the clock and held it to his ear, listening intently, trying to ignore the man's heavy breathing. He could see impatience growing on his customer's face as the seconds dragged by, but some things could not be rushed. Finally, after a full minute, he set the clock down on the counter.

"You certainly do seem to have a problem. I would say that you are losing nearly four minutes every day."

The man's jaw dropped open. "You can tell that just from listening?"

"It has taken quite a bit of practice, but yes. Losing time is a rather common problem with clocks, particularly ones of this age, very often due to accumulated grime or corrosion on the gears. I cannot guarantee anything, but if you come back after four o'clock, I believe I can have it finished."

"Thanks, you're a lifesaver."

The man was halfway out the door, then paused and turned back, a goofy grin on his face. Michael saw the expression and suppressed a deep sigh, dreading what was coming.

"By the way, do you know what time it is when your clock strikes thirteen?"

Michael prepared to play the foolish game, but the man must have been more perceptive than most, reading the resignation playing across his features.

"Heard that one before, I'm guessing?"

"Yes, yes I have."

"No worries. See you at four."

As the door swung shut, Michael reflected on the aborted joke. He had indeed heard it before, four hundred twenty-eight times to be exact. The first had been from his father, who had worked as a watch repairman. Michael, nine years, three months, and seven days old at the time, had taken the question very seriously, proposing answer after answer for two full days before his father finally delivered the punch line. The answer appalled Michael, and he never had found any humor in it.

He pulled himself out of his reverie as several clocks struck the quarter hour. With only four hours and fifteen minutes until the man's projected return, Michael opened up the back of the Bahnhäusle and peered intently at its interior, as did Kronos beside him. *Tsking* at its filthy condition, he carefully began cleaning.

Michael was so absorbed in the task that he did not notice the two young men approaching his door until they burst inside, jarring the bell into a clamorous jangle. As one pushed the door shut, the other pulled out a small revolver.

"Gimme all your money!"

Michael set his tools down with exaggerated care. This was his sixth armed robbery since opening his own shop, twenty-eight years, four months, and seventeen days ago, and he was all too familiar with what to do. Moving slowly, hands clearly visible, he walked over to the register, opened it, and handed all of the bills inside to the gunman.

The youth stared at the small pile. "Where's the rest, old man?"

Michael shook his head. "I am sorry, sir, but I run a small shop, and do very little cash business. Most people prefer to pay with credit cards these days."

Michael could read the young man's expression. Did he have enough time to demand that the safe be opened or not? Michael knew it would do little good; there was less cash left in the safe than there had been in the register. He also knew nothing he said would convince the man of that.

"Come on, we gotta go," whined the lookout by the door.

Beads of sweat began to trace their way down the gunman's face and he chewed his lip, but the pistol trained on Michael never wavered. It looked like he was finally ready to accept the inevitable and leave, when four clocks began to sound Westminster Quarters. The sudden noise startled the gunman, and his finger contracted. His face transformed into a mask of fear as he turned and rushed out of the store, almost knocking over his confederate in his haste.

As he looked down at the crimson blooming across his chest, Michael's first thought was that he would need a new shirt; even if the hole could be patched, the stain would never come out. He took two steps toward the phone before his legs gave out and he landed heavily on the floor, gasping for breath.

Around him, ninety-three clocks began to sound the noon hour.

One…two…three…

Michael counted the strokes automatically, as he had every day for decades. High and low, piping cuckoos and sonorous bongs, the clocks wrapped him in a warm cocoon of sound.

Four…five…six…

They were his friends, his constant companions. And yet, not one of them could do the slightest thing to help him now, beyond counting out the few remaining seconds of his life.

Seven…eight…nine…

Kronos, who had vanished as the men first crashed through the door, padded silently over to Michael, mewling softly, sympathizing in his misfortune, his breath still smelling rather unpleasantly of canned cat food.

Ten…eleven…twelve…

Michael felt the sound crest and dip around him, and prepared to draw his final breath.

Thirteen…and everything stopped.

Michael could still feel the agony in his chest, but beyond his own labored breathing there was not the slightest hint of any other sound. It seemed as if the entire world had gotten stuck between ticks. Angling his head slightly to the left, he could see Kronos bending over him, frozen in mid-sniff. For several heartbeats, nothing moved.

Then Michael heard the bell ring as the shop door opened and closed again. Slow, measured footsteps moved across the floor until they circled the end of the counter, revealing their owner. The man stood moderately tall, nearly six feet by Michael's estimation, though it was difficult for him to judge from his current position. His black hair was short, neatly trimmed and slicked back to frame a long, narrow face, complete with waxed moustache and goatee. He was dressed in a dark crimson three-piece suit, the color broken only by the rose-colored shirt he wore underneath. He did not look a day over forty, but Michael suspected he was far, far older.

"Why, what do we have here? My, my, you seem to have gotten yourself into quite a predicament, friend. Of course, I would be only too happy to offer my services to assist you, should you be willing."

His voice was calm and mellow, with just a hint of southern drawl, but in Michael's ears, it sounded too oily to be sincere, that of a used car salesman turned politician.

"I do not think you have anything to offer that I would want," gasped Michael.

"Is that a fact? Well, perhaps we could start with a little something like this."

He snapped his fingers. Michael instantly felt the pain vanish and his breathing ease, but he was still unable to move.

144

"There now, doesn't that feel better? But wait, there's more, oh ever so much more. I can offer you not only your life for today, but for another twenty years. Think of all you can do with that time, Michael! How many more clocks can you fix in twenty years? How many anniversaries can you celebrate with Kronos here? Or maybe you could attend to something outside of your shop for once. Maybe you could finally patch things up with David."

"David?"

Michael could think of only one person he might mean, but he had to be certain.

"You do remember David, don't you? Your one and only child? I know you've ignored him for quite a number of years, but I don't think even you could have forgotten him entirely. He certainly has not forgotten you, though I must say it was not for lack of trying. In fact, your dear son is even planning on coming here to see you this very next week."

Sadness filled Michael's eyes. "I find that unlikely."

"And I could hardly blame you for doubting it, either, but it may help if you understand that he is not doing it of his own free will and accord. Sarah is forcing him to make the trip. She insists that you need to meet Thomas."

"Sarah? Thomas?"

"Surely you recall the wedding invitation you received a few years ago? The one that David sent despite his better judgment? You decided you were too busy to attend, so you never have met his wife, Sarah. But if you live, why, you'll get to meet her in just a few days. She and David are coming because she wants to introduce you to your grandson."

"My grandson…"

"Yes, indeed. Already three months old and growing like a weed. Of course, if you ever want to have any hope of meeting him, you'll need to survive the next couple of minutes. So, what do you say? Do you want my help?"

"And what will it cost me?"

"I think you already know."

Waves of regret washed across Michael as a thousand thoughts and memories raced through his mind. The joy he had felt, holding David just minutes after he was born, a pure, unbridled joy he had not known since. Missing the first steps, the first words, so many firsts, because they happened while he was at work or, just as often, in his study at home. David crying after he fell off his bike and skinned his leg, his mother tending to the wound and trying to comfort him while Michael lectured him on the mechanics of bicycles and what he had done wrong.

David standing at the door of his study, eyes brimming with tears but refusing to cry, holding the radio-controlled car he had been overjoyed to receive for Christmas only three days earlier.

"Dad?"

"What is it, David? I am very busy right now."

"Can you fix my car? It won't work."

"What did you do to it?"

"Nothing! I was just driving it, and it kind of went down the steps, and now it won't work."

"I will try to fix it," said Michael, "But you need to be more careful with your toys."

That evening, Michael had fixed the loose connection in a matter of minutes, but did not return the car until a full week later, intending to teach David responsibility. It had certainly taught him something. The next time the car broke, David did not even try asking for help. It simply stayed broken.

They saw little of each other once David started school and sports. So many soccer and baseball games missed, so few conversations in the car or at the dinner table. Then the divorce, that unexpected and unwelcome present David had received for his eleventh birthday. Michael's wife had known his habits before they got married, but had always hoped that she could change him, changes that never happened.

Michael moved out and spent even less time with David, barely even noticing if he failed to show up for a scheduled weekend. David was fourteen when he and his mother moved to another city and the visits stopped entirely.

Michael knew he had not done well by his son, not even remotely, but he did love him. It was for that reason he had missed the wedding— not because he was too busy, but because he knew the couple would be happier without him. But maybe it was not too late. Maybe he could finally relate to his son now that David was a grown man and a father, as he never had when David was a child. But was it worth the cost? And could he test the infernal offer, see if the one making it could actually deliver, or if it was just a trap? A thought grew in his head. Perhaps there was a way.

"I will accept your offer, on one condition. I want you to tell me how old I am."

For the first time, confusion and uncertainly flashed across the man's face.

"You want to know how old you are?"

"Yes."

"Well, that should be easy enough," he said, his smile returning. His eyes focused on some point far beyond the wall for a moment before he looked again at Michael. "You are fifty-seven years old."

"Be more specific."

After a sigh and another moment of thought, he replied, "Fifty-seven years, two months, and fourteen days old."

"And?"

"And what?"

"Be more specific."

"And twelve hours and forty-one minutes."

"How many seconds?"

Another loss of focus, this one accompanied by a small frown and a barely visible expression of frustration. After an almost imperceptible shrug, his expression cleared and he said, "Four seconds."

It was wrong. Michael knew, with greater clarity and assurance than anything before in his life, that the answer was wrong. Shaking his head, he sighed.

"I guess you cannot tell me how old I am after all."

Anger filled the face above him.

"Who cares how many seconds old they are?"

"I do."

"Then you are a fool!"

With that, he stormed back around the counter and out the door, producing a discordant clangor from the bell. As the ringing faded to silence, pain once more engulfed Michael's chest, and all around him clocks resumed their appointed task. With every tick, Michael could feel his life ebbing. He used the final remainder of his strength to shift his head, searching the shelf above him.

From his position he could only read the face of one clock, but that was enough. It was 12:02 pm. Michael knew that he was fifty-seven years, two months, fourteen days, twelve hours, forty-two minutes, and...

And...

A voice that was not a voice, but a soundless certainty, filled his mind: *And thirteen seconds.*

For the first time in years, Michael's face blossomed into a genuine smile.

He closed his eyes and with his final breath whispered, "Time to get a new clock."

• 13 •

Aaron Wyckoff was born and raised in Columbus, and other than a few years in Indiana has lived there his entire life. He manages an apartment complex as well as being a freelance writer, editor, and genealogist. In addition to short stories, he enjoys writing picture books and novels for children and young adults.

Acknowledgments

This anthology, like all of Columbus Creative Cooperative's books, was a product of many hands, and we couldn't possibly thank each and every person who contributed to this work.

Thank you to all of the writers who submitted a story for consideration for this anthology. We chose to print only thirteen stories in this book, and we regretfully had to pass on many exceptional stories.

Thank you to our editors, Brenda Layman and Brad Pauquette. You've taken a giant pile of words and turned it into a book.

Thank you to all of the members of Columbus Creative Cooperative who attended workshops to improve each other's work, who share links and forward emails to your family and friends, and who go out of your way to support CCC through the year.

Finally, thank you dear reader. You're the reason we produce books. Without your support of our mission, and your decision to purchase a CCC book, we wouldn't be able to produce the work of Central Ohio writers.

Thank you for taking the time to leave an honest review about our book on Amazon.com or GoodReads.com.

It is with sincere gratitude and humility that we thank the contributors, the editors and the readers for participating in this book.

COLUMBUS CREATIVE COOPERATIVE

Founded in 2010, Columbus Creative Cooperative is a group of writers and creative individuals who collaborate for self-improvement and collective publication.

Based in Columbus, Ohio, the group's mission is to promote the talent of local writers and artists, helping one another turn our efforts into mutually profitable enterprises.

The organization's first goal is to provide a network for honest peer feedback and collaboration for writers in the Central Ohio area. Writers of all skill levels and backgrounds are invited to attend the group's writers' workshops and other events. Writers can also find lots of resources and contructive feedback on our website.

The organization's second goal is to print the best work produced in the region.

The co-op relies on the support and participation of readers, writers and local businesses in order to function.

Columbus Creative Cooperative is not a non-profit organization, but in many cases, it functions as one. As best as possible, the proceeds from the printed anthologies are distributed directly to the writers and artists who produce the content.

For more information about Columbus Creative Cooperative, please visit **ColumbusCoop.org**.

ABOUT THE EDITORS

Brenda Layman is a freelance writer and licensed realtor with Coldwell Banker King Thompson. She writes for *Ohio Valley Outdoors* and *Pickerington Community Magazine*, and her credits include short stories as well as hundreds of articles in both print and electronic media. She is a board member of the Outdoor Writers of Ohio and a member of Ohio Writers' Guild and Satellite Writers of Columbus. Brenda volunteers with Columbus Metro Parks, where she has edited educational materials and nature center displays and installations, including those at Battelle Darby Metro Park. Brenda resides in Pickerington, Ohio, with her husband of thirty-three years, Mark. Brenda and Mark enjoy fishing, especially fly fishing, kayaking, photography, and travel.

Brad Pauquette is an independent web developer and freelance writer in Columbus, Ohio. He lives in Woodland Park, a neighborhood on the near east side of Columbus, with his wife Melissa and two sons. In addition to serving as the developmental and production editor of this project, Brad is the founder and director of Columbus Creative Cooperative. You can find more information about Brad on his website, www.BradPauquetteDesign.com.

OTHER BOOKS BY
COLUMBUS CREATIVE COOPERATIVE

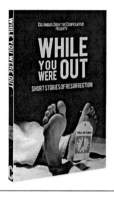

WHILE YOU WERE OUT
SHORT STORIES OF RESURRECTION

Fifteen short stories about people, objects, animals, and even a car, that die and come back to life.

These witty, bizzarre tales will revive your spirit of imagination.

While You Were Out is a 5-star book on Amazon.com! ★★★★☆

Available as a paperback, and as an e-book for the Amazon Kindle, Barnes & Noble Nook and more devices.

Across Town
Stories of Columbus

Twelve short stories, all of which are set in Columbus, Ohio.

If you enjoyed *Columbus: Past, Present and Future*, you will love *Across Town: Stories of Columbus!*

Across Town is a 5-star book on Amazon.com! ★★★★★

Available as a paperback, and as an e-book for the Amazon Kindle, Barnes & Noble Nook, iPad and more devices.

OVERGROWN
TALES OF THE UNEXPECTED

A collection of short stories with a twist.

Overgrown is full of creative, entertaining stories.

Overgrown is a 5-star book on Amazon.com! ★★★★★

Available as a paperback, and as an e-book for the Amazon Kindle, Barnes & Noble Nook, iPad and more devices.

Find more information and order these books and others at
www.ColumbusCoop.org

CPSIA information can be obtained at www.ICGtesting.com
Printed in the USA
BVOW012139170113

310841BV00009B/35/P

9 780983 520580